WOLF POINT

WOLF POINT

A WESTERN DOUBLE

UZZIAH MOUNTAIN MAN
BOOK EIGHT

J.J. BONHAM

Wolf Point: A Western Double

Paperback Edition

Wolfpack Publishing
1707 E. Diana Street
Tampa, FL 33610

www.wolfpackpublishing.com

Paperback ISBN 979-8-89567-359-1
Ebook ISBN 979-8-89567-358-4

WOLF POINT

WOLF POINT

1

Jack Tate had wanted to do this cattle drive because he wanted his own herd on his own property just south of San Angelo, Texas. Now, he was stranded, it seemed, in the far eastern Montana territory with 500 head of prime longhorn stock, two mountain men that he barely knew, a bad chuckwagon cook, and a blind wrangler. He was sitting on the morning of the first day of fall and chuckling to himself. The table that he'd built was sturdy, and the bunks at the other end of the hollowed-out mountain, and the cabin front, which attached to it, was also of the same sturdy construction. He had taken in O.B. Thomas, not so much because he liked him, but because he knew that if Buck took him in, they'd probably kill each other.

Buck Krieter was a good man, basically, but the way he whined and whimpered over the forty-some barrels of whiskey which the Blackfeet and the Crow had destroyed, you'd have thought they were members of his family. It took him three weeks, but he finally dried out —sorta. It had been rumored that Uzziah had bought a bottle of bonded whiskey off a paddleboat captain, the same one who had brought Brownley up here, and Buck was pestering the poor mountain man to death for a drink.

Whatever! The summer had been good to the stock, yes, they'd lost a few—well, forty to the wolves and coyotes, but at least there weren't any bears this far east in the territory. At least, they hoped not.

They figured out a way to make an early warning system for the wolves, and so far, the wolves had not figured it out.

They strung empty bean cans, any kind of cans they could get along a wire or string, and when the wolves passed through that area, the cans would clatter and the rifles and the men would come from their nearly underground living quarters and bang away at them. Surprisingly, the younger the wolf, the more it tasted like chicken. *Doesn't everything,* thought Tate, but the older wolves tasted more like pork. As the season would progress, all of those there would find that the wolf would have become a staple in their diets.

Tate had built his cabin/underground-place on the hill east of where Uzziah and Immanuel had built theirs, and now he could see Uzziah standing in the doorway, and Uzziah saw him and waved. Tate waved back.

"Do ya trust Jack Tate?" Uzziah asked.

"Guess, as much as I trust the next man, I mean, we are in this so-called business together."

"So, ya don't trust him."

"Did I say that?" Immanuel asked, coming to the wide door, and seeing Tate out there chopping wood.

"No, but ya didn't say ya did trust him."

"I didn't, yer right. 'Member that old saw, *Love many, trust a few, but always paddle yer own canoe?*"

"No, thankfully, I don't," Uzziah said and turned and went back inside to get himself another cup of coffee.

"I think I heard it from ya first," Immanuel said, turning in the doorway and looking back at Uzziah.

"No, ya didn't."

"Think I did."

"Well, ya was wrong like again, if ya knows what I mean," Uzziah said sipping the brew, satisfied, he came back out and walked through the door to the table they had built for the porch—well, it was just an area they leveled off with shovels they bought, but it was nice to sit out there when the flies weren't so bad. The breeze kept them away, as opposed to the cabin, where they seemed to live on forever.

"Come on, sit, and we can discuss the rest of our faithful crew," Uzziah said, sitting and pushing the other chair out with his booted foot.

"Let me get some more Joe," Immanuel said. He'd heard Jack Tate refer to coffee as Joe, and he liked the term.

Uzziah watched Tate working with the wood. He swung the axe good, and his leg, the one he'd broken badly when the longhorns stampeded, looked like it had healed nicely. In fact, Uzziah had to stop and remember which leg it was, he was walking on both so good.

Immanuel came out with his steaming cup of Joe, and he had a catalog from some company called

Tiffany's Blue Book. He was thumbing through it when he sat down and looked at Uzziah.

"What's ya thinking 'bout orderin'?" Uzziah asked.

"Well, how much of the money we found in the tent do we have left?"

"That is a secret."

"From them, it is, I get that, but come on?" Immanuel asked.

"Enough," was all Uzziah would say.

"So, ifn I wanna buy a new gun—"

"Ya don't need a new gun, here, let me see, what kinda gun is it?"

Immanuel handed him the catalog, and Uzziah looked at the picture.

"It's purty, and Samuel Colt makes it," Immanuel said hopefully.

"Forget it, by the time we'll need something like a new gun, this picture will be down the shite hole and buried."

"Hey, lookie yonder," Immanuel said, and as they both looked, they could see the familiar smoke from a paddle wheeler, "I didn't think one was due so soon."

Uzziah went to the barn and saddled up Shadow and Stygian. Immanuel was getting stronger, and he had put on both weight and strength in the summer, but Uzziah just liked doing things for the older man.

"I told ya to stop saddling my horse fer me," Immanuel said, objecting, but not really.

They both mounted up and rode to the dock at Wolf Point, which had been rebuilt. The paddle wheeler was still some time away when Jack Tate rode up.

"Ya guys gonna buy some more stuff?" Tate asked.

They both knew he had more money than they did, and was hiding it as well, or better, than they were.

"Nah, we just come down to see the tourists," Immanuel said.

Tate just looked at him, and turning his horse, rode back to the ranch, which was spread out over nearly forty acres, at least the fenced-in portion was.

"Wouldn't hurt fer ya to be more accommodatin', ya know," Uzziah said.

"Yeah...no, I don't know," Immanuel said as one of the sailors from the paddle boat jumped onto the dock and started flinging wood up to the boat. The captain walked down, they didn't know this particular captain. Well, they were about to meet him.

"Hey, you the fellas that keep this Wolf Point wood station stocked so well?" he asked, looking between Uzziah and Immanuel.

"Yeah, well, there's five of us, but we do most of the chopping," Uzziah said.

"Can't tell ya how much the company 'preciates it, in fact, got this token from the company," he said as he walked down the gangplank and handed Uzziah an envelope. It was fairly thick, and depending on the denominations of the bills, it could be a nice sum.

"Thanks," Uzziah said without looking inside.

"Well, winter's round the corner, so, this will probably be the only payment till spring, but ah, hey, don't ride off, we got a passenger onboard who is staying till we come back this way," the captain said, and as he finished the sentence, both men looked up to see a Catholic priest in a long clerical cloak walking down the steps and from the upper decks, he had a couple of valises with him.

"Father De Smet!" Uzziah nearly shouted as he got off Shadow and ran up the gangplank to help the older man with his bags. He had grown older, just as they all had. He was still walking straight and tall, and his face was clean-shaven. The smile on his face belied the many trials and tribulations that he'd undergone in his ministry.

"Brothers!" he shouted at the top of his lungs. "It's been since the Mormon winter quarters since we've seen each other, hasn't it?"

"Why? What?" Uzziah only managed to get out.

"Don't worry, I'm not moving in, it's just I thought I'd come and visit some old friends, although, perhaps we never were really friends, eh?"

"Nonsense," Immanuel said as he, too, had gotten down and was tying the father's valises onto the D-rings of Stygian.

"My, my, I do remember your fine black horses, and I am so glad that no harm has come to them," De Smet said.

"Jump up here with me," Uzziah said, extending his arm down for the Father to grab and swing up behind him.

"Wait," De Smet said, then he turned his attention to the paddle oat captain. "Don't forget, even if I'm not on the dock stop, I will come running," De Smet said and laughed.

The captain waved as they rode off, and soon, the steam whistle from the paddle wheeler was blowing screams, and both horses picked up their speed as they made their way toward the ranch.

De Smet was hanging on to Uzziah firmly around the waist, and his eyes were taking in everything he saw.

"Take me around and show me the ranch," he said to Uzziah's left ear.

"He wants to see the ranch," Uzziah yelled over to Immanuel, who nodded and changed direction.

They rode past the corrals that they had sectioned off as best they could for the cattle. They had the mother cows and the calves in one such corral, and others contained different combinations of the cattle.

"Longhorns?" De Smet said.

"Yeah, driven up from Texas," Uzziah said proudly.

"That's excellent. I hear they do well in cold weather like all cows."

"Well, that's good," Uzziah called back to the man.

They rode the ranch, and Father De Smet got a good look at everything that was going on there. When they passed the chuckwagon, Buck was sitting on the buckboard seat and eating breakfast.

"Father De Smet, this is Buck Krieter, he was the chuckwagon cook on the drive," Uzziah said.

De Smet put out his hand, and Krieter shook it.

"Pleased to meet ya, Father. I can't tell ya how long it's been since I been to confession or mass," Krieter said, evidently feeling he had to say something about the man being a priest.

"Well, we shall take care of that while I'm here, young man. Your immortal soul is important to God, and he wants you with him when you die," De Smet said.

Krieter started getting choked up and his voice croaked as he tried to speak. "Father...those words... they're so...kind," was all he could get out.

"Well, I didn't mean to spoil your breakfast. We'll talk more later, okay?"

"Yes, Father, thank ya," Krieter said.

Uzziah clicked up Shadow and the two men rode off on him. Once they were a distance from the chuckwagon, the Father spoke up.

"I'm surprised he isn't a Jew. Lots of Krieters are Ashkenazi Jews who lived in the Rhineland before they migrated toward the Slavic countries."

"How do ya know such things?" Uzziah asked.

"Too much reading, I tell you, I need to stop reading so much," De Smet said, then added, "He must dig, as you and this other house there, and get inside the hills before the winter comes. He will not survive well in the wagon in the winter."

When they got back to the boys' cabin and dismounted, Immanuel spoke up. "I'll put the horses up," he said, and Uzziah handed him the reins to Shadow.

"I like what you've done here," De Smet said, admiring the way the cabin had been built into the hillside. This will help the temperatures inside the cabin remain more or less constant without using too much wood," De Smet said.

The Father looked and saw that there were only two beds in the place, in the back and close to the fireplace.

"Don't worry, I can sleep right in front of the fire, as a matter of fact, as I was growing up, that's where I'd sleep, no matter what bed they put me in, in the morning they would find me by the fire."

Uzziah had seen Tate riding around, checking fences and doing what had to be done on a ranch. Tate had seen they had a guest, but maybe the cleric outfit put Jack Tate off, who knew?

Once the Father got settled in and he and Immanuel were having a coffee and a smoke at the outside table, Uzziah made up his mind.

"Hey, I'm gonna walk over to Tate's, invite him over fer supper. Him, Thomas, and Buck. Be right back," Uzziah said as he started walking the hundred yards or so across the fields and past some of the corrals. As he approached Tate's cabin, he came walking out from the barn he'd built.

"What's up?" Tate asked.

"We have a visitor."

"Yeah, saw that."

"I'm gonna cook supper tonight, and I'd like you, Thomas, and Buck to come over and eat with us."

"I don't take to clerics too much," Tate said while he opened up the door to his cabin.

"He's a lot more than that. Heck, twenty years ago he was in the Bitterroot Valley in far western Montana, and he knows a lot 'bout Injuns, cattle, a whole bunch of things. Don't not meet him simply because ya don't care for priests."

"Well, I'm livin' with one, yeah, and what he done while he was a priest, well, it don't set well with me, and if he ever gets drunk agin and starts in on all he done and how he done it, I swear!"

"That would actually be a good thing fer ya to talk to De Smet 'bout, course not when Thomas was there. By the way, where is he?" Uzziah asked, looking around.

"He's down at the river, fishing. His luck is something else, want me to bring some fish to the supper?"

"Well, ya think he'll catch any?"

"Hey, the man charms 'em out of the water, ya just

fix everything else and we'll bring the fish, okay. I don't have the luxury of shunnin' somebody 'cause they serve God, just had my fill lately," Tate said, actually trying to be nice.

"Good, good. The winter's comin' and this is yourn herd more than anybody's. Immanuel and I don't lay no claim on yer beef, ya know that, right?"

"But ya felt fine about giving away half of it to the Injuns!"

Uzziah figured this was what it was all about. It wasn't that he didn't like priests, well, maybe with O.B. staying with him, he'd grown tired of one sinning priest, but the feelings Tate was having weren't about any of that. It was all about Immanuel and Uzziah giving the longhorns to the Crow and Blackfeet.

"Say, ya know ifn we hadn't done that, well, they would have simply come back later and taken what they wanted, ya know that, don't ya?"

"Yeah, yeah, I know, I know."

"And they wouldn't have cared who they harmed when they were doin' that. Immanuel and I know 'bout the plan that ya had with Brownley, and that weren't exactly right, but Brownley must have been a twisted soul, the way ya tell it. Now, we're stayin' here this winter fer one reason and one reason only, to help you and whomever ya can get eventually to ride herd on these cows to bring 'em to market next summer. We ain't gonna take any monies, we're just gonna help ya out, 'cause—ya know..."

"Ya stampeded the longhorns and almost got all of us kilt," Tate put it quite simply.

Uzziah looked at him and realized how bad he still

felt about what had happened when the cattle stampeded.

"We shoulda come up with a better plan, but we didn't," Uzziah finally said.

"Okay, okay, O.B. and I will be there. Ya gonna ask Buck yerself?"

"Yeah, I'll drop by the chuckwagon and talk to 'im," Uzziah said, then added, "Later."

As Uzziah was walking over to where Buck had sort of permanently parked the chuckwagon, he saw Buck with his homemade fishing pole, leaving the wagon.

"Where ya goin'?" Uzziah asked, and Buck held up the pole and line.

"We're havin' supper fer the Father, come on over 'round suppertime, and we'll feed ya."

"I'm tryin' to get Thomas to teach me how he fishin' like a fool, he always gets 'em." Buck said, then added, "But I'll be there, and I'll bring O.B.," he said as he ran off toward the Missouri.

The day was blustery, and the winds had brought in some clouds from the west. They were black and promised heavy rains, which was good for the prairie grasses and the ponds that they had dug out around the cattle.

The longhorns were looking west, where lightning strikes were producing no thunder that could be heard, but still, it looked like a shite show further west. Maybe the storms would play themselves out and would skirt right by them.

2

That evening, while the sun was way up, it always seemed to stay up longer in the Montana summer, Uzziah had put together some venison steaks on the grill outside and, before that, had prepared a big pot of hominy grits, some fresh field onions with dandelion greens, and, of course, his johnnycakes and biscuits.

Father De Smet had sat outside with Immanuel, who was grilling the venison, and they seemed to be talking easily, or at least it seemed that way to Uzziah, who was inside cooking in the big fireplace. He had himself a pot crane which held several arms that could be brought on the fire, then brought to the side to keep whatever was cooking at a simmer, or simply hot. It was a good arrangement, and Immanuel had made it for him. He thought, when they got back to the cabins, he would take this back to the mountains.

They had set a long table out in front of their dugout cabin, and there were plenty of tin plates and cups to go around. All in all, Uzziah had counted everyone who would be there, and it looked like he'd be serving only six people.

Uzziah heard some talking, actually, a lot of fast talking, as if someone were happy and surprised, and when he looked out, there was Blind Thomas, as they were calling him now, all smiles, shaking hands with Father De Smet. Immanuel was placing on the grill the fine fish that Thomas and maybe Buck had caught. Buck was right, though, there was no one luckier than Blind Thomas in knowing where along the banks of the Missouri to fish.

By the time Uzziah brought out the crock of grits and the johnnycakes, biscuits, and the field greens, everyone was sitting around the long table, and their appetites seemed up.

Father De Smet stood at the head of the table.

"Gentlemen, if you don't mind, please join me in prayer. Father, for these and Thy other gifts, we are eternally thankful," he said, then he crossed himself and kissed his thumb.

Uzziah knew how to do it, even though he wasn't Catholic, because a neighbor boy in the Shenandoah Valley had told him an easy way to remember the crossing of the body. The boy had told him, *Go to your head, remembering that's where your spectacles were, then to your groin because that's where your testicles were, then to the left side of your chest because that's where your wallet was, then to the right side of the chest because that's where your watch was.*

It was easy—spectacles, testicles, wallet, and watch!

Uzziah had noticed Immanuel trying to copy the good father, but Blind Thomas and Buck, who must have been Catholic, were right on cue. Jack Tate didn't join in the prayer, close his eyes, or even try to cross himself. *Maybe he was a heathen*, Uzziah thought.

The talk was lively as it always was when the food was being passed around, and once everyone had what they wanted, the talking ceased as men ate as men do, in silent seriousness. As the meal was winding down, Father De Smet spoke up again.

"I'm in doubt," he said with his French accent. "Which was most delectable, the fish or the venison?"

"The brown trout are my favorite," Blind Thomas said.

"How can ya tell they're brown?" Tate asked, and everyone laughed.

"When ya draw them from the waters, they feel different than the rainbows and certainly there's no mistaking a brown for a carp," Thomas said.

Uzziah looked at Immanuel. They had discussed how Blind Thomas had become brighter and perhaps even a better person since he'd lost his sight. He never again talked about the violations of the young women in his parish, and they certainly hoped he would not talk about them this evening with Father De Smet there.

There was probably little chance of that, since there was hardly any whiskey left, and certainly no other alcoholic beverages. It seemed that when men drank, their tongues were loosened, and things which more than likely should not have been talked about were.

"Well, you wonderful gentlemen have treated me to this meal, so fabulous, *tres bien*!" he finished in French. "And now, I have brought along a treat for all of you," he said as he went into the cabin and brought out a bottle of red wine.

The sighs and groans around the table told the tale

of how long it had been for these men to have tasted such luxuries.

"Now, this merlot, I only have five bottles, but one must be saved for the communion, the Holy Sacrament that I will host on Sunday, but now, we can enjoy just a taste, no?"

The coffee that was in the tin cups was summarily tossed to the ground, and then the cups were stuck out for the merlot.

"Now, gentlemen, tomorrow I will hold confession to all who would like to, I might say, indulge, if that could be said about confession. But if you are Catholic—"

"This is like one of them places that makes ya listen to a sermon before ya get yer meal, huh?" Jack Tate said, standing up.

"Jack, sit back down and show our guest some respect, will ya?" Immanuel said, and he was starting to stand, until Uzziah grabbed his arm and pulled him back down.

"For Christ's sake—" Jack said, but was interrupted by Father De Smet.

"The wine for Christ's sake will be served on Sunday at the Eucharist," the priest said, smiling.

Uzziah couldn't help but admire the unflappable priest and wanted to cheer.

Tate wasn't as impressed and threw down his tin mug on the table and started to walk away when Blind Thomas spoke up.

"Jack, even a blind man can see that yer not gonna get any wine, unless ya act civil."

"To hell with civil," Jack said.

"But you might want to hear of the market I already

have for your beef, at least the ones you're willing to share at this point," De Smet said, then added, "And it wouldn't be bad to recoup some of the monies you've obviously lost in the trail ride up here, would it?"

Tate hadn't gotten very far from the table, maybe twenty feet. He stopped and he turned around. "Is this a joke?"

"I started a herd of longhorns in the Bitterroot Valley several years ago. The Flathead and Salish Indians needed meat, and it worked well for them, but rustlers have been stealing the cattle from the mission and taking them across the big hole to where there seem to be burgeoning gold and silver mines. The miners must eat, but stealing cattle that don't belong to them is not the way to do it."

Tate was interested now. There seemed to be a market for his longhorns, a ready market at that, and then there were the rustlers who were—to be exact—the same ilk as he and the others who had stolen the longhorn herd for Brownley, who was now dead.

"What's gonna keep them rustlers from stealing the cows I sell the mission?" Tate asked.

"These two men right here," Father De Smet said as he put his hands on Immanuel and Uzziah's shoulders.

Immanuel looked at Uzziah like *what the hell is this sky pilot talking about*, but Uzziah just smiled and whispered, "I'll tell ya 'bout it later."

"So, you two are gonna drive the cattle they need at the mission all the way across the Montana territory, sell them, then return to give me my money?!? No way! I don't know ya two from Adam, and after yer rescue of us at the watering hole, I wouldn't let ya take a calf across the river to be sold!" Tate yelled.

"No, that's not what I had in mind," De Smet said, then added, "I'd like Immanuel and Uzziah to go to Bannock and find out who the rustlers are, and deal with them. You, Jack Tate, I want you to take your own cows to the Bitterroot and sell them to the mission. They can raise them and make money selling them to the miners, but these cattle don't need to be taken until the rustlers have been taken care of, do you understand? God willing, that will be in the spring."

"I don't believe in God," Tate admitted, raising his head a bit.

"That's okay, my son, God believes in you," De Smet said, and Buck started to cry.

"What ya blubbering about!?!" Tate asked Buck.

"That's so beautiful, what the Father said. I ain't heard nothin' like that since I was in Catholic school, when I used to think it was hogwash, but Jack, come on, we made it through that awful stampede, the Injuns helped us get chere, and our so-called boss was kilt by them, but they's friendly to us, how can that be nothin' but God's doin'?!" Buck went on.

Everybody at the table was looking at Buck, the one man that they never expected to say so much, especially so much about an eternal being who created us all. De Smet and Uzziah were beaming, it seemed that the priest had gotten through to one man and gotten through in a big way.

Jack Tate didn't know what to say or do until Father De Smet picked up the tin cup Jack had thrown down, and pouring a generous amount into the cup, approached the man and extended it to him.

They had gotten through the better part of the four bottles, and everyone was a bit lit. Uzziah looked over at Immanuel, who seemed about as peaceful as he had ever seen the man.

"Maybe ya need to switch from whiskey to wine, old son?" Uzziah asked Immanuel under his breath. That was okay, no one would have heard, the others were busy laughing at the stories De Smet was telling about when he first encountered the Flathead and Salish Injuns and the times they had understanding each other. Tate was laughing the hardest, it seemed that he had gotten beyond the fact that he didn't believe in God. Perhaps it was De Smet's comeback about God believing in Tate that had finally turned the corner for the man?

By the end of the evening, De Smet had gotten Tate to agree to the bargain. Well, it turned out that De Smet had certain specified monies with him that he had been authorized by the Catholic Church to pay for beef if he found any. It seemed the church was not willing to lose its foothold in the Montana territory, no matter what.

Everyone parted company that night, Buck making sure and telling the father that he would be at the confessional tomorrow. Blind Thomas had also said something to De Smet, but no one was sure what that was. They were all relieved that he hadn't started in on his violation of the virgins at the church he'd served at.

Once everyone had left and Father De Smet had lain down in front of the fire and was almost snoring before he got settled, Immanuel turned in his bed and whispered to Uzziah.

"Is we gonna get Buffalo Warrior to help us with the drive?"

"I guess it's the only way. My worry is that it's so close to fall that we could get caught in an early snowstorm," Uzziah said.

"Yeah, up chere, I don't imagine that that would be very purty," Immanuel said.

The next morning, they were up early, as they always were, but Father De Smet had already beat them up. When Uzziah was making coffee, he looked out the window of the cabin, and there was De Smet, talking with Buck across the way. Maybe this was going to be the way he was going to do the confessions among those who wanted them.

"So," Buck said, looking at the priest, "ya wanna use the chuckwagon as a confessional?"

"Well, it's away from everyone else's cabin, and I'd only need it for a few hours. I can put a tarp up between the two sections, and it will work fine," De Smet said.

"Can I go first?" Buck asked.

"I'm not supposed to know who's in there, Mr. Krieter, you know that, right?"

"I know, but with so few of us, ya'd know, wouldn't ya?"

"Let's make it for the afternoon, when it's warmer, okay?" De Smet said without answering Buck.

Uzziah had breakfast ready when Father De Smet got back from his own personal tour of the ranch. They sat down at the table in the cabin.

"May I bless the food?" De Smet asked.

Both the mountain men bowed their heads after the three men joined hands around the table.

"Father in heaven, for these and the other gifts, we are eternally grateful." Uzziah was about to let go of De Smet's hand, when the priest continued, "I know that these men are not Roman Catholic, but Father, they are men, men who have sinned in the manner in which they have led their lives, not knowingly sometimes, but still, things have been done which cannot be undone, but can be forgiven. We pray all this in the name of Thy son, Jesus Christ, Amen."

They passed the food around, the usual fare from Uzziah's kitchen and they ate. De Smet had a good appetite for an older man, and between the three of them, they ate everything that Uzziah had fixed.

"I'm having a space arranged for me to hear confessions this afternoon," De Smet said, sipping his coffee.

"Buck's chuckwagon?"

"Yeah, it'll work well, I think."

"I ain't a Catholic, so what good does it do me to tell you what I've done wrong?" Immanuel asked.

"There are things which we do as life progresses, and some of those things are not easy to bear, forget, or, for that matter, forgive ourselves for."

"Yeah, so, that's life, right?"

"Yes, Immanuel, that's life without absolution, but there's something not really mystical, but rather common about telling another man the things you've done which are not stellar in your life. Something about sharing which allows you a space where you feel you can get some absolution, some relief from what you've done," De Smet finished and looked at Immanuel, who seemed deep in thought.

"Hey, partner, 'member when we left the courthouse in Chicago, how we'd been cleared of the crime which we had been accused of—the killin' of that poor Robert Spells?"

"Yeah, sure, but we didn't kill 'im, wasn't that the whole point?"

"But what 'bout the cowboys, the wranglers who died when we stampeded that herd?" Uzziah asked.

"This ain't the confessional, Uzziah, is it?" Immanuel asked.

"He's right, let's leave it alone. The opportunity will be there, and who knows, if you come and talk with me, you might feel a liberation of sorts, or maybe not?" De Smet said.

De Smet decided to move the confessional to the next morning as he realized. He asked Uzziah and Immanuel to let everyone know.

3

De Smet was an older man, and he went to bed a lot earlier than the two mountain men. That night, they could hear him snoring while lying by the log fire. It was nearly the end of summer or the beginning of fall, whichever way you wanted to look at it. This Montana territory had a habit of being cold when you thought it would be warm and warm when you suspected coldness.

They were comfortable, allowing for layers and long johns to make up for whatever the weather presented. Layers could always be unworn, peeled away, or brought back into play.

"I ain't gonna talk over nothin' with the Father," Immanuel said.

"Even after he went to all the time to explain everythin' to ya?"

"Say, how short is yer memory, huh?"

"Whatcha talkin' 'bout?"

"The last time I confessed anything, it got writ up in a newspaper by the scribbler, and it led to us having bounties put on our heads, and just the thought of that month we spent in that Pinkerton jail cell back in Chicago, well, it gives me the willies, it surely does."

"Ya know he's taken an oath not to tell what ya say?"

"Yeah, well, he can keep the damned oath, I ain't sayin' shite 'bout nothin' and that's that."

"Okay," Uzziah said and packed his pipe again, and lit it up.

"What 'bout ya?"

"What 'bout me?"

"Ya confessin'?"

"Nah, I got a direct line to the real Father, why should I talk to a man when I can talk to the son of God?" Uzziah said, blowing smoke that got caught and taken back into the cabin.

"Yeah, what ya said. Besides, talkin' with God, that's prayer, right?"

"Well, sure it is."

"God's not gonna rat on us, is he?"

"Immanuel, sometimes, ya amaze me. Who would God tell that would do us any more harm than God hisself?"

"That a trick question?" Immanuel asked, grabbing the coffee pot off the small fire they had outside and pouring both him and his partner a fresh cup.

"No, my friend, it is not. Once we told God, we don't hafta tell anybody else, that's the only confessional we need, trust me on this, okay?" Uzziah said, patting Immanuel's arm that rested on the table.

Immanuel looked down to his arm that had just been patted.

"What do ya do things like that fer?"

"Like what?" Uzziah asked.

"Do ya think touchin' me on the arm is comfortin' to me?"

"I have no idea, would ya rather I didn't?" Uzziah asked, looking at Immanuel quizzically.

"Nah, I do like it, sometimes, I think I like it too much," Immanuel said, looking away to where the last of the sun's rays were shooting up from the west.

"I will care fer ya, and take care of ya, as long as we are alive, my good friend, never worry 'bout that," Uzziah said as he turned his face away from Immanuel.

"We ain't gonna go separate ways, is we?" Immanuel asked, putting his hand on Uzziah's arm.

"Stand up, fool!" Uzziah said as he stood.

"What's up?" Immanuel looked at Uzziah and couldn't figure out what was going on.

"Get up, fool!" Uzziah reiterated.

Immanuel stood and was in a crouched position as if he might have to protect himself. Uzziah reached out and grabbed Immanuel, who was ready to rumble if that's what was going to be going on.

"We're brothers, ya know," Uzziah said as he held out his arms.

"Okay," Immanuel said, not knowing what to do.

"I love ya," Uzziah said as Immanuel's eyes got big.

"Ya ain't gettin' the dash-fire fer me, is ya?" Immanuel said, stiffening.

Uzziah pushed him away, "Ya wish!"

"I do not, it's just—ah hell—I love ya, too, ya old bastard. Ya done drawn the long bow on me again, ain't ya?"

"No, I'm not tellin' stories outta school. I just figure,

before either of us takes the earth bath, well, we should know where we stand," Uzziah said.

"Yeah, well, afore I lays down the fork and knife, I will stand by yer side, no matter what," Immanuel said.

"Are you going to kiss each other, or am I watching all this for nothing?" Father De Smet said he was up on one elbow and looking at the two men in the doorway.

"Stopped acting like an unlicked cub, ya ole scally-wag!" Immanuel said to the priest as he closed the door on the cabin.

They could both hear Father De Smet laughing inside the cabin.

In the morning, it was still early, but neither of the partners had rolled out of their beds. Uzziah heard it first, probably because his hearing was better. There was someone crying, really bawling, and when he swung his legs to the floor and pushed his boots back on, Immanuel looked from his bed.

"What the hell's all that bawling? Is one of the calves stuck somewhere?"

Uzziah didn't answer, but went to the door, opening it, he stood there and listened. The noise was coming from Buck's chuckwagon, and as he watched, Buck himself dropped from the back of the wagon, and his hands went to his face, and it was his tears and his crying out that had broken the morning. Not just for Uzziah and Immanuel, but the front door to Tate's cabin was open, and Blind Thomas was walking toward Buck. Well, all he had to do was follow the sound of the tears, which were enough to break any man's heart.

Uzziah watched as he was joined by Immanuel, who was looking over his shoulder.

"What the hell?" Immanuel said.

Thomas found Buck, who grabbed the blind man like he was a life raft, and the two men hugged in the early morning dew that still covered the grasses. Tate shouted something that could not be understood from that distance and slammed the door to his cabin. Meantime, Buck was rocking back and forth in the arms of Blind Thomas, who was cooing, that's what it sounded like, cooing.

"What the hell is this all about?" Immanuel finally asked.

"The confessional," Uzziah said, and went back inside and started to make coffee.

"Really?" Immanuel made a face, then walked out of the cabin and across the field where Blind Thomas was holding Buck.

He walked up to them, and when Buck looked at Immanuel, he slugged him in the face, and Buck went down.

"Now, ya have somethin' to cry 'bout!" Immanuel said as he turned and walked back to his cabin.

Back at the cabin, he added a couple small logs to the dwindling fire. The sun was breaking the horizon now, and the day would be warm, but not yet.

Uzziah and Immanuel were sitting there enjoying their coffee when there came a knocking at the cabin door. Immanuel picked up a pistol and held it beneath the table.

"Come on in," Uzziah said, and when the cabin door was opened, Blind Thomas and Buck came in.

Buck was acting sheepish, and Blind Thomas was smiling.

"Ya got coffee?" Blind Thomas asked, already smelling it from across the glen.

"Sure, pull up a chair, Tom," Uzziah said.

Buck followed him like a puppy and took the first cup of coffee that Blind Thomas poured. He could do it by putting his index finger in the cup, and when the liquid reached his finger, he stopped pouring.

Buck sat down at the table and couldn't look at anyone. Blind Thomas joined him and began talking.

"Buck's got something to say to both of ya," Blind Thomas said with the most beautiful smile on his face.

Buck looked up, almost surprised that Blind Thomas had said what he'd said.

"I gots to go with cha," was all Buck said.

"Where we gonna go?" Immanuel asked Buck, who looked right at him.

"To kill them bastards that are stealing the priest's cattle," Buck said, and burned his mouth taking an enormous gulp of coffee.

"This what De Smet told ya to do?" Uzziah asked.

"Hell no," he's a man o' God, and heard me tell him all the wrong I done for the past fifteen years, and man, there was a lot, and the more I told, the more that came to me. My soul has been washed clean in the blood of the lamb, and now, I'm gonna do pertinence," Buck said, sipping the coffee now.

"And killin' the rustlers, which by the way, you were not less than a few months ago, killin' these rustlers will do that fer ya?" Immanuel asked.

"It will, brother," Buck said, looking Immanuel right in the eyes.

Uzziah sat back, took a deep breath, and let it out.

"BT, tell me what ya know?" Uzziah asked.

They had started using his initial instead of wasting so much breath.

"I know this man's done with being evil and now he wants to do good," Blind Thomas said.

"And killin' those rustlers will do that fer ya, huh, Buck?" Uzziah asked.

"It will. Ain't no other way. Father De Smet done saved my soul—I mean—a course that it's Jesus that saves, but he done opened the door, and Jesus flooded in, and now, I'm gonna kill for good," Buck said, holding out his mug for BT, and by God, Blind Thomas took it, and poured more coffee for him. How the hell did they do that?

They went about their chores for the rest of the day. There was simply a certain amount of care that had to be taken with the longhorns. Uzziah would see Immanuel working, throwing dried grasses into corrals, and they would nod back and forth. Blind Thomas had his chores also. They were mostly seeing to fences, and he did this by walking along, and dragging his gloved hands along the rails and or wires, and when something seemed out of the ordinary, he fixed it. His work on the fences was good, steady, and most of the time, most, it didn't have to be redone.

Jack Tate had wandered over to the chuckwagon and was standing outside. It seemed like he was talking to De Smet, but would not go inside. Who knew? Tate stood there a long time, and finally, De Smet opened the canvas on the back of the wagon and said some things to Tate, who bowed his head while Father De Smet prayed. This whole business with the Jesuit priest was turning out in some peculiar ways. Uzziah figured they were only peculiar to those who didn't do that sort of work. Obviously, Tate had confessed, who knew?

That night, they had a big supper at Tate's, and De Smet cooked. He did some fairly fancy cooking when you considered it was all over an open flame. In a frying pan, he melted bacon grease and made a version of sole meuniere, with herbs that he'd gathered in the fields around the ranch. Evidently, the priest had brought potatoes with him, and they were placed in the outside of the fire and baked, some too much on one side, but with the fish, and the wine, well, he did have more wine after all. He had a dry white, a pinot gris, and a sauvignon blanc, which went well with the fish. Blind Thomas had outdone himself in the fishing department, although he gave lots of credit to Buck for being a quick learner.

They ate all the fish, all the potatoes, on which they drizzled bacon bits and grease, and De Smet had brought along some Swiss chocolates, which were small, but when passed around with the fresh coffee, they made the ending of the meal fabulous.

As they sat around the table that had been dragged outside for the supper, Tate spoke up.

"I'm sending a letter to my wife back in Texas, pretty close to Belknap, it is. Little town called Carlton, Texas. After we get the longhorns to both the miners, the mission, and the last of them to Cheyenne, then I'm gonna go get her and bring her up chere. She and her sister, Molly. Gnomes, Harry, was my nephew, her son, and I gots him killed on the trail drive. Anyway, Father De Smet has encouraged me to make amends to her, and my wife, and get them up chere, so that's what Imma gonna do," Tate said, and that was that.

No more was said about those plans as they finished up the wine, and Tate brought out a bottle of whiskey, which Uzziah hated to see, but was surprised when Immanuel waved the bottle off, and didn't have any.

On their way back to the boys' cabin, they were walking easy through the tall grasses and De Smet spoke up.

"Boys, I can't tell ya how well this has all worked out," he said, and even in the gathering darkness, Uzziah could feel Immanuel looking between the two other men with him.

"We leave tomorrow for Wisdom," Immanuel said to the Father, for it was the small town of Wisdom in the Montana territory that was halfway between the Bitterroot Mission of Father De Smet and the placer mining fields near Alder Gulch. The Father had surmised that's where the rustlers were hanging out. "And when ya see us again, we can pretty much guarantee that no more cattle will be rustled from the missions."

4

The exciting thing about any trip for Uzziah was the fact that there were so many unknowns. Yes, they had a good idea of where they were going and a fair notion of whom they might encounter along the way, but still, there was the element of the unknown. This element gave a certain tingling to getting ready for the trip, saddling up, mounting up, and riding out. What lay ahead was a mystery, and Uzziah liked that.

"So, how do ya plan on dealing with the rustlers?" Buck asked.

Uzziah and Immanuel looked back and forth. Rustling was an offense punishable by hanging, and they fully intended to use the punishment.

"Whacha suppose we should do?" Immanuel asked the chuckwagon cook.

"I don't know, what's yer plans?" Buck asked again.

"Maybe we could bring 'em back to the ranch and they could help with the chores, once they know they been caught?" Uzziah suggested, winking at Immanuel.

"Yeah, yeah, many hands make an easy job," Buck agreed.

"'Course, yer probably agreeing with this cause yer a rustler, right?" Immanuel said right to Buck's face.

"Well, that were different," Buck suggested.

"How?" Uzziah asked.

"Yeah, fill us in on that. Ya got hired by the poor bastard who didn't know ya was gonna double-cross him, then ya started killin' off the real wranglers, oh, and by the way, ya accidentally poisoned the man who was the trail boss, the man who had hired ya, the only man who knew where the watering holes were, and ya fed 'em rattlesnake poison, ain't that right?" Immanuel asked.

"What is all this? I thought ya'll done forgave us for those things," Buck whined.

"No, that were God, and the padre, we ain't forget nor forgiven, young son," Immanuel said.

"Well, that ain't fair," Buck complained.

"Ya got any rattlesnake poison, on ya?" Uzziah asked.

There was a pause before Buck answered.

"That means he does," Immanuel said, pulled Stygian up, and, sitting his horse, looked at Buck.

"What? What?" Buck wanted to know.

"Either ya hand the poison over, or we search ya," Uzziah said.

"And ifn we find the poison, we'll hold yer mouth open and feed it to ya," Immanuel chimed in.

"I ain't got any poison on me!" Buck objected loudly.

"Fine, then after we search ya and find none, we'll believe ya," Uzziah said.

"Ain't we got a long trip ahead of us, ain't we supposed to be helping Father De Smet out?"

Immanuel drew his revolver and cocked it. It was pointed right at Buck's midsection.

"This ain't right!" Buck protested, then, without warning, he kicked his horse up into a run.

"Uzziah, get 'im off that cayuse, will ya?" Immanuel said, pulling his pipe from his vest and loading it.

Buck was looking back, thinking he could outrun Shadow, which was not going to happen. Fairly soon, Uzziah had his lariat out and was circling the loop overhead, and when he threw it, Buck had just looked back again, and it caught him around the left arm and the neck.

Uzziah whoaed Shadow and Buck came flying off the backend of his horse. He hit the ground hard and rolled around, moaning.

"Ya search his person, I'll search his saddlebags," Immanuel said as he rode past Uzziah, who was dismounting, and went after Buck's horse.

Buck didn't carry a sidearm, and the rifle he used was still in the boot on the saddle. Uzziah walked up and took the loop off Buck.

"Ya coulda kilt me, ya damn fool!" Buck complained from the ground.

"Get up, empty yer pockets on the trail, and do not make a false move," Uzziah warned him.

"We're wasting valuable time when we could be helpin' the padre, and ya know it!" Buck was still caterwauling about his predicament.

Uzziah fired the Hawken right over Buck's head, his cowboy hat went flying.

"What the hell!" Buck screeched.

"Everythin' on the trail, yer pockets turned out!"

"Look what he's doin' to my stuff!" Buck shouted, pointing down the trail where Immanuel had emptied out Buck's saddlebags, and everything was lying all around.

"Now!" Uzziah said as he started loading the Hawken. "Ifn I get this chere Hawken loaded afore ya done what I asked, yer dead!"

Buck knew Uzziah was serious, he was throwing stuff from his pockets on the trail and digging as deep as he could through his vest, his coat, and everything was hitting the ground.

"That's it!" Buck shouted as he threw his hands into the air like he was trying to win a calf roping contest.

Immanuel came riding back, "He's clean, ifn he has some it's really well hidden," he said to Uzziah.

"Yeah, nothin' chere, neither," Uzziah said, and mounted back up. The two partners rode away.

"Ain't ya gonna wait on me, fellas?" Buck asked as they kept right on riding. "Sons of bitches! Damn them mountain niggers!" Buck swore.

Down the trail and not looking back, Immanuel looked over at Uzziah. "Ya think he'll take a shot at us?"

"Well, ifn he does, it'll be the last time he tries to backshoot somebody," Uzziah said with a smile.

About half an hour later, Buck rode up, his horse was heaving, and he was still angry.

At first, neither partner said anything to Buck, who rode abreast with the other two men, but soon, he realized he was imposing on them and dropped back. The morning was chilly for late summer, and there were clouds in the west, but it looked like a good day to get on with it.

They didn't speak to Buck, nor he to them, until that night when they made camp.

"Yer cookin', right?" Buck asked Uzziah.

"Yeah. So far, I ain't poisoned anybody, at least not yet," Uzziah said as he set up to cook them supper.

Buck just shook his head and mumbled something under his breath. They ate, and were sociable enough. Buck didn't say two words, and for the next three days, it was like that. They were making good time and were almost to the Yellowstone River. They were traveling southwest so that they might find the river and travel along it until they got to the Gallatin Range, where there was purported to be a pass over into flatter land that would lead to the Big Hole Basin, which was the highest and widest of the broad mountain valleys. It was halfway through the Big Hole Basin where Wisdom lies.

They were along the Yellowstone River and having fished that afternoon, Buck brought about a dozen—they ranged from longnose suckers to cutthroats and some redside shiners. He had been thoughtful enough to clean them down by the river, and when he got to camp, well, Uzziah figured he'd catch something, so he had grits, johnnycakes, and beans boiling. All that remained for them to do was grill the fish.

As the fish was getting done, and it never took long, there came two riders from across the Yellowstone.

"Hello the camp!" one man shouted, and the way they were backlit from the setting sun, it was impossible to see them well.

All were ready in the camp in case these two were

the scouts for a larger band of renegades or outlaws. As they approached the camp, the White man spoke up.

"I'm Osborne Russell, and this chere Injun—"

"We know him!" Uzziah said.

"We do?!?" Immanuel asked. Uzziah had known for some time that Immanuel's vision was failing him, but he didn't want to say anything.

"Heavens yes, that there is Abooksigun," Uzziah said, and before he could go to the two travelers, Immanuel was over there shaking hands and talking them up.

"Come on, we got more fish than we could ever eat," Uzziah said.

"Ya trust that Injun?" Buck whispered to Uzziah.

"More than I do you," Uzziah said right out.

They were squatting around the fire, which was warming them in the cool of the evening. There were so many questions that Uzziah and Immanuel wanted to ask their friend, but it wasn't accepted to tell private things to folks who weren't familiar with other people's relationships. True, Immanuel and Uzziah had fought with Abooksigun, and even visited with him up at the land of burning ground, but whatever they had to say to each other could be said later.

The meal was greatly appreciated by Russell, who said he was looking for a pass between the eastern and western territories that would allow for easier travel. He'd come upon Abooksigun and the Injun had basically come along with him, and he wasn't sure why. They turned in after that, and Abooksigun and the two mountain men sat around the fire longer and smoked their pipes.

"Thought ya was gonna stay until ya figured out

what the bubbling paint pots was tryin' to tell ya?" Immanuel asked.

"I figure," Abooksigun said in his matter-of-fact way, then changed the subject. "Bad medicine has been on you," he said, looking at Immanuel.

"He looked worse before this," Uzziah said.

"Don't apologize fer me," Immanuel said. "I had some trouble with the drum in my chest," Immanuel said.

"You mean heart?" Abooksigun asked.

"Yeah, my heart."

"White men paint the red man like child. It not drum, it beating muscle in chest."

"Well, ya haven't changed," Immanuel said.

"I am who I am, and if not mistaken, God said same to Moses."

"You're right, and I guess I shouldn't be surprised," Uzziah said.

"Made us in image and his children."

"When did ya become a biblical scholar?" Immanuel asked.

"Listening to those paint pots, winters long, Rahab give Bible."

"Did ya know that?" Immanuel asked Uzziah.

"Doesn't surprise me. She was all about spreading God's word," Uzziah said.

"So, that still don't explain why yer up this way?" Immanuel said.

"One sick, not sure which one? Hear two bear men bring longhorns, and a bad man, soul like moonless night."

"Ya can't keep any secrets up this way!" exclaimed Immanuel.

"You know black soul?" Abooksigun asked.

"No, we only saw his tortured and dead body," Uzziah said, remembering the way Brownley had died.

"That is good. What do with body?"

"We buried it right down from where he was hangin'," Immanuel said.

"Stay away, no bury any near," the wise Injun said.

"Still don't explain why yer up thisaway," Immanuel said.

"You need my help."

"Okay," Immanuel sort of said low and looked at Uzziah.

"Ya know what we're up to?" Uzziah asked Abooksigun.

"Both yes and no. Had dream, many people, squaws, little ones, and plenty bad hombre. We not go stumbling forward," he said and smiled.

Uzziah and Immanuel looked at each other and smiled.

"What we do must be secret, and mysterious," Abooksigun said.

"Why?" asked Immanuel.

"Powerful people want too much when stop, want scapegoat," Abooksigun said, loading his pipe again and lighting up.

"Powerful how?" Uzziah asked.

"All their souls like moonless night. They must be wiped out, all of them, even the women and children," the Indian added.

"There's womens involved in this?"

"Yes, once when younger, men dressed as women to rob, now men who commit crimes have squaws, babies. Crush or will continue."

"We ain't killing no babies," Uzziah said quite matter-of-factly.

"Not kill in death, but kill to those who know them," Abooksigun said.

"Whatcha mean?" Immanuel was curious now.

"Squaws and babies scattered, raised as Crow, Blackfeet, Arapahoe, Cheyenne, and Sioux."

Uzziah and Immanuel just looked at each other. They didn't know what to think. Why was this necessary? How would it be accomplished, and that was just the start.

"Ya know how we can do this?" Immanuel asked their Injun friend.

"I do. Will end where it ends, and go no further," Abooksigun said, then added, "Must close eyes, tomorrow, talk," he said, and he went over to where he'd spread his blankets and rolling up in them and went to sleep.

"What in God's name is going on here?" Immanuel asked Uzziah.

"Got no idea, brother, but we'd better pay attention to him, after all, he's been listening to paint pots bubble, right?" Uzziah said, moving over and curling up in his bedroll.

Immanuel sat there, feeling as if he'd just stepped onto a different planet. There were rustlers, but instead of just killing, hanging the rustlers, they were to take their families, mothers, daughters, and sons, and sprinkle them among the nations. Why? What good would that do? He thought about his own circumstances, how he'd been fathered by a White man, and left there in the village of the Mandans, then taken by the Sioux, then on his own. Yes, he'd grown up and loved his Mandan family, but was that better than being rescued by his father, Patrick Gass, and living in Baltimore?

Then, he thought about his stepmother and the way she had acted toward him when he was in New Orleans. What would it have meant if he had slept with her? What would that have done to his White father? How would that have affected his White brothers and sisters, or, for that matter, his Mandan family? Too many questions were swirling around in his head, and the answers were not coming. It was best for him to simply go to sleep and see what Abooksigun had in mind.

5

The next day, Osbourne Russell said his goodbyes to Abooksigun and went on his way looking for an easier passage to the western Montana territories. Uzziah had fixed breakfast, and Buck was looking at Abooksigun in a strange way.

"This one mad?" Abooksigun asked.

"I ain't mad at ya," Buck offered.

"Mean crazy," Abooksigun corrected himself.

"Who ya callin' crazy!" Buck said and was over at Abooksigun when he felt a Bowie knife at his throat. "Sorry, sorry, sorry, I gets excited sometimes."

"Crazy, this one," Abooksigun said again and went back to sopping his gravy with the last of his biscuit.

They traveled the rest of the day, going south and west along the Yellowstone River to its sources in the Rockies. They crossed the Continental Divide, where the snow was already gathering for the winter, and went on down and toward the beginning of the big hole area. It took them about a week because of the snow, and they were all glad to get back to flatter ground. Then they came up to Big Hole River, which led eventually to Wisdom. They gathered supplies at a crossroads of sorts.

The settlers who helped them out did not like the look of their crew, and when they originally showed up, there was some confusion.

"Hello, the cabin!" Immanuel shouted out, and a woman came from the cabin. She had a child on her hip and a dishtowel in her hand.

"This ain't the place," she said with a heavy Irish brogue, then pointed northwest. "Ya foller the Big Hole River 'bout fifty miles. That's the place," she said and started to go back inside.

"Yeah, we know the place," Uzziah wisely said, then added, "but we come up short on supplies, wonderin' ifn we can camp chere tonight, and use yer barn fer cover?"

"I don't like tellin' a bunch of men and an Injun that I'm alone, but I am. My husband works at the place yer goin' and he ain't chere," she continued talking in her Irish accent, and stepping back inside where she exchanged the dishtowel for a Greener. She did not hesitate to show how many of them she could cover with it.

Uzziah took some gold coins from his purse and threw them down near the entrance to the cabin.

"Just give us some bacon, beans, and maybe flour, and we'll be on our way," Uzziah said.

"And coffee!" Immanuel reiterated.

"Don't want much, do ya?" she scolded the grown men, never taking her eyes off Abooksigun.

She went back into the cabin and everybody stayed mounted, afraid that she might unload on anybody who got down. She wasn't gone five minutes before she threw a gunnysack into the yard, such as it was.

"Now git!" she said, pointing the scattered death at everybody.

They rode on down the Big Hole River about ten more miles, didn't want her thinking that they might be coming back, and made camp.

Sitting around the fire after Buck cooked supper, they talked.

"That's the last time that man cooks fer us!" Immanuel said.

Buck just looked down at his hands, which were holding the meager fixings he'd called supper.

"Truth be told," Abooksigun said.

"What ya know, Injun!?!" Buck scowled at him.

"You no cook," Abooksigun said.

After they ate, everyone's stomach was so upset that the four of them headed out toward Wisdom. They figured if they rode hard and didn't stop except to water and rest the horses, they'd be there the evening of the next day.

Buck's horse had a time of it, and he was having trouble keeping up. The morning of the second day, they could see the ranch that was called Wisdom. The river ran right past it, and it was big. There must have been twenty horses that they could see, and a barn that could hold more. They crossed over to the other side of the Big Hole and camped down in a bog, where they couldn't be seen. Of course, Buck didn't know they'd forded the Big Hole, and he rode right on into the ranch.

"That son of a bitch is walking up to the ranch door," Immanuel said as he was spying through the glass.

"Maybe that good," Abooksigun said.

"And maybe it ain't," Immanuel said.

"Let me see," Uzziah said and took the binocs from Immanuel.

Buck wasn't stupid, but he was misinformed. He knew they were going out to the Big Hole to a place called Wisdom Ranch and deal with some rustlers. Well, hell, he was a rustler before and all, and when he lost the three men he was traveling with and then saw the ranch house, he just rode on in.

Inside the ranch house, cowboys lazed around the big fireplace, doing what cowboys do. Some were drinking coffee, some whiskey, and some were actually reading. The newspapers they had they'd gotten in and around Alder Gulch, where placer mines were beginning to pay out.

There were couples there, that is to say, some of the cowboys/rustlers had their families at the ranch. Women were clearing the table of the supper things, and children were running around playing. All in all, there were about thirty to forty people in the big room. Bedrooms lined the balcony on the second floor, and there was a big staircase that went up there on both sides of the big room.

As mentioned, the fireplace was blazing, and the fruits of their ill-gotten gains seemed to be working out for all of them.

The fields where Immanuel, Uzziah, and Abooksigun were hanging around had cattle with a lot of different brands on them. One brand stood out above all the rest, it was a circle with a cross in the middle. The brand of Saint Mary's Mission, in the Bitterroot Valley, about a hundred miles away. A little far for that many of the mission's cattle to have wandered, not to mention the pass they would have had to come over to get here.

"This is the place all right," Immanuel had said before he spied Buck walking up to the front door.

There came a knock at the ranch house door, and everyone froze in place. They never locked the door or put out sentries because this hideout was so far from anywhere that they just didn't feel a need.

Finally, someone drew a gun, while others drew theirs and sent the women upstairs, and the one who had first drawn opened the door.

"Howdy!" Buck said as if he was expected for Sunday dinner.

Everyone got up from where they had been sitting and walked to or around the front entrance.

"Who the hell are ya!?!" the first cowboy asked.

"Buck Krieter," he said, extending his hand for a shake. Someone grabbed the arm that the hand was connected to and flung Buck into the house, and a couple of cowboys ran outside to see who was with this uninvited stranger.

They ran around outside making sure their horses were secure, looking in the barn and all around, and finally coming back into the house. When they did, Buck was seated on the hearth warming his hands.

"Buck, what are ya doin' chere?" a man asked in some sort of accent. Buck thought he'd heard that sort of talk before, but couldn't remember where or when, then he remembered it was the small cabin right before they got here. He was in his fifties, and he looked, well, like he might be the man in charge.

"Are ya the trail boss?" Buck asked the man, once again sticking his hand out for a shake.

"Yeah, yeah, I am, names Bronson, Kirk Bronson," he said in an Irish brogue, and he actually shook Buck's hand.

"Nice to meet ya, Kirk."

"Well, I takes care of the cows, but the real boss is yonder," Kirk said in his brogue, "That there is Amsterdam Vallon."

"Can ya explain yer presence here at our ranch?" Vallon asked.

"Yeah, sure, I'm with another bunch of rustlers over in eastern Montana territory—"

"Yer what!?!" Vallon said, putting a revolver under Buck's chin and cocking it.

"Look, I always found it's best not to beat 'round the bush, ya know?"

"Uh-huh," Vallon said without removing the revolver.

"My pards and I stole 1500 head of longhorns from the man who bought them. Got them over at Wolf Point now."

"There ain't nothin' at Wolf Point," someone in the crowd of cowboys said.

"There is now," Buck said confidently.

Another cowboy, looking like he might be the second, walked over and whispered something to Vallon, who lowered the gun and uncocked it.

"Say, I'm Charlie Bledsoe, and I done heard some rumors 'bout what yer sayin'."

"No kiddin', well, good news travels fast, don't it?" Buck said, smiling.

"So, humor us, Buck, that's yer name, right?" Charlie asked.

"Yeah, yeah, sure is!"

"Why would rustlers across the state who have a herd want to make contact with other rustlers, not saying that we are rustlers, but why would that happen, can ya tell us that?"

"Say, mind ifn I had a swig or two of that, is that Irish whiskey there?" Buck asked, and everyone in the room, including the women who were hanging off the balconies, laughed heartily.

"Well, it sure ain't Irish moss! No, no, we certainly don't mind," Charlie said, and he had someone hand him the bottle. After Buck took a couple of good shots, which got the crowd of cowboys whooping at the size of them, Buck started in.

Sometimes, a good man is never known for a good man until the time comes for him to reveal himself. What Immanuel, Uzziah, and the others who had herded the longhorns all the way from Colorado didn't know was that Buck was a natural-born storyteller.

He started in at the bar in Belknap, Texas, and went from there. When he got to the thirsty dying longhorns along the front range, a few of the others had joined him in a drink. He had them on the edge of their seats, and when he told the part about the mountain men who had stampeded the cattle back toward the watering source, and the way the cattle smelled the water, and their horses, too, well, you could have dropped a pin and it would have been heard.

As the cattle rammed into the legitimate wranglers and they were sent to hell, and Jack Tate had had his leg broken and Blind Thomas had somehow—maybe through the smartness of his horse—every cowboy wanted to believe in that. After all, being with a horse all day long, it paid to think of the creatures as smarter than yourself.

Well, the cowboys were up and hollering, and whooping and cheering, and Buck wasn't even in the Montana territory yet.

The two partners and their Injun friend, Abooksigun, had expected to hear some gun firing and maybe even see them bring a rope out to hang Buck from the hook extended out from the hayloft. But none of these things happened. Instead, over the course of the next hour or so, the crowd of cowboys inside were shouting and hollering, and whooping, and it really seemed as if there might be a party inside the ranch house.

"What the hell!" Immanuel said, then added, "Sounds like they's rollin' out the red carpet fer our cook!"

"What ya think's goin' on?" Uzziah asked Abooksigun.

"He trickster, different than first thought," Abooksigun said.

"Whatcha mean trickster?" Immanuel asked.

"He drunk."

"What?" Uzziah nearly shouted, but it wouldn't have made any difference with the way the party was going on the other side of the Big Hole River.

"He tell story, they like," Abooksigun said.

"Great, the rustlers are being told a bedtime story," Immanuel said.

"Yes, they get drunk, sleep, good," the Injun said.

Uzziah and Immanuel looked at each other, then Immanuel spoke, "Ya got to go see what the setup is over there, young son."

"Me?"

"No, I look, better me," Abooksigun said, and before they could say anything, he'd slipped from their presence and they could hear him swimming the Big Hole River.

"Guess that's decided, then," Immanuel said.

They tried to rest, but it was cool and damp in the bog, and they wanted to hear what their Algonquin friend had to say. It was about an hour before they heard Abooksigun sloshing back toward them.

"What's it look like?"

"Squaws, papooses above it all. Let's make stampede."

Neither Uzziah nor Immanuel wanted to do the stampede thing again. They had done that out on the plains at the front range. It had been a disaster, many wranglers hurt, killed, Jack Tate's leg broken. And now they were thinking about stampeding the stolen cows—that was crazy, but they didn't have a better plan. Abooksigun said there were at least thirty cowboys, wives, children, and there were three with Buck. Drunk, he was definitely drunk on the inside. But then again, so were the rest of the cowboys, or most of them. Abooksigun noticed about three wranglers who weren't really drunk, but they would not be enough to stop three hundred head.

First, they would have to get the herd to ford the river to where the big cabin was. Obviously, the rustlers had put them over here to graze, so the stolen cattle would remember where they'd forded, where they'd crossed before, and they just needed to needle them down to that spot, have them cross over, then fire up the stampede.

6

They were about to start the cattle across the Big Hole River when a voice sounded out. When they looked with the spyglass, it was Buck, and he had his hands on either side of his mouth and he was making it loud.

"Hey, Uzziah Ferguson O'Bannon, ya need to come on over chere right now and talk, and like now!" Buck yelled.

There were several cowboys standing on either side of Buck, and they were armed with rifles.

"He done gave us up, that's what he done," Immanuel said. "Imma gonna kill that s.o.b. the first chance I gets."

They mounted up their horses and forded the river. It looked like those who had gathered outside were more surprised by Abooksigun than they were the two mountain men.

"Come on down, nice and easy like," Bronson said, then added, "Which one of ya is O'Bannon?"

"That'd be me," Uzziah said as they took his

weapons away from him, including the Bowie knife. Uzziah looked over and they'd disarmed Immanuel except for the knife he kept in his boot. Uzziah reminded himself that he would have to start carrying such a weapon. Abooksigun seemed nonplussed by all that was going on, he voluntarily gave up all his weapons, and when the men at the big cabin saw the tomahawk, they went back and got tomahawks off Uzziah and Immanuel, which were under their long coats.

Back inside, the warmth of the fire felt good. Abooksigun went over by the fire because he'd forded the river to spy on them, and sat there steaming, his deerskins giving off clouds of moisture as he dried out.

Uzziah and Immanuel were told to sit in two chairs near the fire. The men there, and the women on the second floor, looked at them with a great deal of suspicion, as well they should.

"I'm Amsterdam Vallon, and these are my Dead Rabbits," he said, gesturing to the men, women, and children surrounding him.

"I'm Uzziah Ferguson O'Bannon, and that's my partner, Immanuel James Jones—"

"An English name fer sure!" someone in the crowd of men shouted, and there was a din of boos.

"And this is our friend, Abooksigun," Uzziah finished up.

Vallon turned to Abooksigun. "Ya wouldn't happen to be Choctaw, would ya?"

"Can be, if need be," Abooksigun said, and there was a smattering of laughter.

"What tribe do ya originate from?" Vallon asked.

"Algonquin."

"Which ones, the Mohegan, Pequot, Narragansett, Wampanoag, Massachusett, Nipmuc, Pennacook, Abenaki, Maliseet, or Passamaquoddy?"

Abooksigun sat up and looked differently at Vallon. "So, you know differences?"

"Sure, I'm from New York City and did business from there with all the Algonquin tribes, and you are?"

"Maliseet," Abooksigun said.

"Good farmers and better trappers," Vallon said and put out his arm, and he and Abooksigun did the arm shake that Injuns like.

Vallon turned to Uzziah then, "And where do ya hail from, brother Irishman?"

"The Shenandoah Valley."

"So, yer a farmer, too, good then ya'll understand our tale of woe, perhaps. First, yer partner there needs to stop looking at Buck as if he wanted to kill 'im. Mr. Krieter has done ya nothin' but good charms and much luck—"

"I'll be the judge of that!" Immanuel said.

"I'm sure ya will, Englander, but keep yer yap shut while I spin ya a yarn, will ya?"

Uzziah looked at Immanuel as if to say, *Please*.

Immanuel nodded to Uzziah, but that was good enough for Vallon.

"It was a while back that my father, Priest Vallon—"

"Yer pa was a priest?" Immanuel asked.

"I'll get to that, can ya keep yer partner quiet? I got a tale to tell? Anyway, Priest Vallon was an Irish

Catholic who came to New York during the Great Blight. The potato crop was failing, as it would continue to fail for almost ten years. The bloody English built poor houses for the Irish but they were no more than places where those who were starving to death could go and be out of the sight of the bloody English who had all they wanted to eat—after all, they owned the land which rightfully belonged to the Irish, and they let us serve them by farming the land, but once the Blight happened, all that changed.

"Me pa was a good man, and we did what we did in Ireland, we stole. After all, when ya have to steal to eat, well, is that really stealing? He formed a gang in the Five Points area of New York and we was organized like ya couldn't believe. We wasn't tryin' to get rich, ya understand, but we was sending monies back to Ireland so that those poor bastards who were starving to death could have enough money to buy bread and something else to stay alive.

"We were naturally opposed as it seems we are the world over by the Protestants, who had a gang called The Natives. They was run by William Poole, who, I am aghast to tell ya, eventually kilt my pa in a final confrontation between the two gangs, one Irish Catholic and the other Catholic hating Protestants.

"The two gangs met, and it weren't the first time. The Natives called us Irish barbarians, and me pa had already cut out one of William Poole's eyes and left him to live in shame, but no, Poole reorganized, and there was a final battle to decide who would rule the Five Points. It was a cold day, and the snow, which was soon to be splattered with the blood of both Protestant and Catholic alike, was everywhere. For a while it looked like we would win, but somehow a one-eyed Poole, kilt his way to the middle of the Dead Rabbits, and stuck my father with two knives. The Dead Rabbits, seeing their eventual demise, fled the scene. William Poole stayed there, and I was there in the background and witnessed the whole thing.

"As he approached my father's body, he did an awesome thing. My father was beggin' him to end his life with a final stroke of a knife, and Poole spoke to him. I'm not sure what he said, but as he rose from the body, he inserted the long knife into my pa's heart and started ending his life. But he took that same knife and placed it in the hands of Priest Vallon, so that he might have a weapon on the other side to fight his foes.

"As the Natives fled the scene, I crawled up to where my pa was dying. He looked at me and said, 'Don't ever look away.' I took that to mean that as he died, he wanted me to see him die, but later, I realized he didn't want me to ignore the plight of the Irish, either in the Five Points or during the famine in Ireland.

"A lot of the things we stole we sold and got money to send back to Ireland, and since I've moved out here, there has only been one thought in my mind. How can I best serve those who are dying in Ireland right under British rule?

"This rustling has been an answer to my prayers. We steal cattle, sell them to the miners over near Alder Gulch, and most of the monies, we send to Ireland."

Uzziah and Immanuel had listened in deep respect to the story told by Priest Vallon's son, Amsterdam Vallon. But now, a deeper truth needed to be revealed to the man.

"Ya've been stealin' from St. Mary's Mission in the

Bitterroot Valley, haven't ya?" Uzziah asked the leader of the rustlers.

"Aye, we have. The cattle are little protected and the pickings are easy," Vallon said, smiling.

"But don't ya realize," Uzziah said, "that ya've been stealing from Peter to pay Paul?"

"Aye, but Peter has more resources than Paul, and shouldn't brothers share?" Vallon asked.

"They should, but we are friends with Father De Smet—"

"The priest who started the mission?" Vallon asked.

"Aye," Uzziah said, falling back into the Irish way of saying yes, "and we have been sent by the good Father to stop the rustling of the cattle."

Amsterdam Vallon looked perplexed. He got up and walked around the room. When he came to Abooksigun, he put his hand on the Algonquin's shoulder.

"Ya know it was the Choctaw who gave us this idea, don't ya?"

"No," Abooksigun said.

"Oh yeah, those Choctaw, they been sending monies to Ireland in support of their Irish brothers, and do ya know why?"

"No, why?" Uzziah asked.

"Because they see within their history a repeating of the abuse of the Irish by the English. They were forced to move in their trail of tears from their southern homeland to the Indian territories, and they are smart enough to know that this type of manipulation by the forces that be, regardless of whether their English or American just means that those with money and power are controlling those without.

"I was in New York City when I found this out, and

thinking of American Indians sending monies to help starving Irish brothers, well, it gave me the idea of doing something out west that would help more than stealing watches in New York City."

"And I agree, I had no idea about the Choctaw, but I agree, this selling of cattle to send monies is a good idea, but yer stealing from the Salish Injuns to do it," Uzziah said.

Vallon was perplexed and caught in the middle of his stealing ways. He didn't know what to say.

"Two wrongs don't make right," Abooksigun said, "it takes three wrongs."

Everyone just looked at Abooksigun like he was crazy.

It seemed a tragedy of possibly the greatest magnitude had been avoided. And who had done the due diligence, but a drunken man who was a lousy cook. The boys decided that they would spend the night outside. The big cabin was full, and there were a lot more women and children than they had dreamed. Abooksigun joined them once they'd built a fire and started a pot of coffee.

"Irish have strong medicine," Abooksigun said, sitting down Indian style beside the fire.

"Do not give this man any ideas. He's already thought that he was bulletproof," Immanuel said.

This seemed to interest the Algonquin Injun more than just about anything that had been said that night.

"When did bullets avoid you?" he asked Uzziah, who looked at Immanuel.

"Go ahead, tell him."

"It was when I was with the Mormons, I met a man named Porter Rockwell—"

"I hear of this man," Abooksigun said.

"Impossible," Immanuel said.

"Protector of big White medicine man, no?"

Uzziah looked at Immanuel.

"How do you know that?" Immanuel asked, pouring the coffee that was ready into three tin cups he'd retrieved from his saddlebags.

"The salty lake his home, now," Abooksigun said.

"You've been up listening to paint pots for the past few years!" Immanuel protested.

"Visitors," was all Abooksigun said.

"Visitors, visitors, like the land of vapors is some tourist attraction!" Immanuel said.

"Will be," the Injun said.

"Yeah, yeah, will be, but who came by and saw ya when ya was up there?"

"Spirits," Abooksigun said.

"Spirits?" Uzziah asked, now getting involved with the talk.

"One lady with little boy."

"No, no, no, we're not goin' there!" Immanuel said.

"What'd she look like?"

"Nice."

"And the boy?"

"Your son," Abooksigun said.

"No! No!" Immanuel screeched.

"Ya guys okay?" Someone from the house stuck their head out the big cabin door.

"Yeah, yeah, we're fine," Uzziah said.

"Ya done talked to him, haven't ya?" Immanuel asked, looking at Uzziah.

"No, no, why would I?"

"I no talk, upset everyone," Abooksigun said and sat back.

"I'm gonna sleep on this whole thing. What we almost did, what we done afore, and how we were about to do it agin, I don't know, Uzziah, it's tired me out completely," Immanuel said as he curled up in his bedroll, and before Uzziah poured another cup of coffee for Abooksigun, he was asleep.

"Tell me 'bout the spirit visitors," Uzziah whispered to Abooksigun.

The Injun looked at Immanuel and started in. "She come to me, tell story of rescue."

"Yeah, that was something," Uzziah said, remembering her rising up out of the coffin and the way the Comanche ran for the hills.

"No tell him?" the Injun asked, pointing at Immanuel, who was snoring loudly now.

"No."

"Spirit world not his."

"I know."

"Your world, Uzziah, you move there," Abooksigun said.

"Do I?"

"Your mother make sure."

"What ya mean?"

"She give you medicine to move there."

"How?"

"Not meaning to, just did."

"What do I do with that?"

"Be there."

"But how?"

"Every brave has his path."

"And mine?"

"Walking it now."

"But..."

"Trust this," Abooksigun said and leaned forward, and Uzziah thought he was going to hand him something tangible, but all he did was touch Uzziah's chest right above his heart.

"We were about to do some bad medicine, weren't we?" Uzziah asked his Injun friend.

"Thinkin' not doin'."

"The drunk saved us."

"Once in council with chiefs, big problem, a brave, not a chief, speak loud outside teepee. All chiefs looked and wished he not speak. But he did," Abooksigun said.

"And?"

"His words led us."

"And it was random, right?"

"No. Spirit world speak through all things," Abooksigun said, finishing his coffee and dumping the dottle from his pipe into the fire. It flared up and was gone.

Abooksigun nodded and wrapped into his blankets.

"She come," he said with his back to Uzziah.

"What!? Who?! Hannah?" Uzziah whispered to Abooksigun, but there was no answer.

That night, Uzziah had a dream, it was short and it was sweet. Hannah appeared to him. She had a small child by the hand, and he was the age George would have been if he had lived. She was gesturing for him to follow her, and as he did so, he realized they were at the spot on the Missouri right about where Wolf Point was. They walked together, he taking her hand, and there were many houses, many more, and they were filled with the children and their ma's and pa's.

There was a celebration going on, and Buck emerged from his summer home of the chuckwagon, and there was a woman with him, and she was pregnant.

The dream ended. Uzziah awakened and got up on one elbow. The fire was down to smoldering coals, and over the big cabin, a moon was rising. *Buck with a pregnant woman*, Uzziah thought, then the thought occurred to him, *Why not!*

The man, the no-good drunk, who couldn't cook, the man they had discounted all along, had saved them from making a murderous mistake, and that must be honored. Uzziah vowed to pay more attention to everything anyone said, anything anyone did. They were all messages from a world in which his friend, Abooksigun, had told him he existed simultaneously with the so-called real world.

Then, he remembered his ma taking him down to the school that had existed for a while in the Shenandoah Valley. It was called Ceries School. She would drive the buggy down there to the school, and he saw that all his brothers and sisters had successfully gotten out of the wagon and run into the school. He would turn to his ma, and she would say, "*What are ya gonna do today?*"

He would answer, "*Be more Christlike.*"

7

It was decided the Irishmen who had been stealing cattle to send monies back to Ireland for famine relief would go with the trio—Abooksigun, Immanuel, and Uzziah. They would take the cattle to the man who had bought stolen cattle from them before, his name was Con Kohrs. He had been wintering in the Blacktail Creek area, and when the miners started in for sure in the spring, he would need more beef.

Their plan, well, all of them, really, was to sell the herd they had before winter, at market price, he'd been getting them a lot cheaper before, seeing how they were rustled, but now since most, if not all the Irishmen's herd was branded with the Mission of Saint Mary's brand, Uzziah assured them that the beef was legal since they were representing Father De Smet and the plan all along had been to stop the rustling, and that's exactly what they were doing. The monies from Con Kohrs would be split between Father De Smet and the Irish relief fund, and the Irishmen would then work for

Jack Tate and help with the raising and selling of legitimate beef.

As they began to move out, one of the dogs that belonged to Amsterdam Vallon whelped pups. She was an Irish Wolfhound named Rosy, and all Wolfhounds were great hunting dogs that could run down a grown deer, and were often many times greater than the size of a timber wolf. They stopped while this was going on, and Amsterdam came back from the bushes where it was happening and had some bad news.

"She's dead," Vallon said.

"What happened?" Uzziah asked.

"She had these two big'uns, then expired," Vallon said, uncovering the two newborn pups he was carrying in his arms.

"What'll happen to them?" Uzziah asked.

"Well, without their ma to give 'em milk, they'll die, might as well wrap 'em up in a gunny sack and throw them in the river," Vallon said.

"No!" It was Immanuel, and he had gotten down off his horse. "We'll raise 'em up, won't we, Uzziah?"

Uzziah was in shock that Immanuel had shown interest. First of all, he wasn't known as a great lover of dogs, but also, how would they do that?

Immanuel turned to the two wagons that had all the women and children in them, at least the women who didn't have their own horses.

"Is there a milkmaid among ya?"

"I'm a milkmaid," a middle-aged lass said as she stuck her head from the wagon.

"Will ya do the favor for the Irish Wolfhounds?"

"And what favor would that be?"

Immanuel took both pups, one a male and the other a female, and walked over to the wagon.

"Can ya nurse these two?" he said, holding the little blind things up.

She looked at first with disgust, then a change came over her.

"Are they toothless like a baby child?" she asked, and the other women in the wagon made groaning noises, "Ya shut up, the lot of ya! I nursed all yer babes after mine died, and now, they're nearly all weaned. So, shut up!"

"Yeah, takes 'bout three weeks afore they get teeth," Immanuel said, and once again, Uzziah was wondering where all this information came from.

"I'll do it," she said, taking them both into the wagon, then turning after she set them down. "But it's gonna cost ya, big!"

"Can't thank ya 'nough," Immanuel said, and he took some coins from his purse and handed them to her.

"More than that, lad!" she reiterated.

"They survive, ya name yer price," Immanuel said as he mounted up on Stygian and the party took off.

They stopped at the little house, where Charlie Bledsoe's wife was stored, and his kids, two of them, a wee girl and boy, not more than six, the oldest. Charlie had thought that trouble might come their way, and he'd made the house far away from where trouble might land.

"What are ya sayin', Charlie?" she asked in her

strong Irish brogue. "I'm to leave the house we built, and take up the children and go off with ya, agin?"

Charlie got down and went to her. She was standing in the doorway, the way she had been when they were bartering for supplies. Uzziah wondered if she would pull the Greener on Charlie, but instead, she pushed him away, slammed the door, and threw the lock log down.

"She's not comin'?" Vallon asked.

"Ya know Meg when she gets this way," Charlie said, then louder so that she could hear, he said, "We'll just leave 'em here and pray to God the winter and the savages don't get them."

Charlie Bledsoe mounted back up and they started on down the road toward Alder Gulch. It wasn't five minutes before there was a caterwauling which filled the air as Megan Bledsoe drove her buggy after her husband, the whole time, she and the two children crying.

"Good God, Bledsoe, do somethin'," Vallon said to the man.

Charlie rode back and tying his horse to the back of the buggy, got in and drove, while Megan and the kids gathered around him, simpering.

"Now that is not an advertisement for marriage," Vallon said.

They rode along and Vallon, Immanuel, Uzziah, and Abooksigun were heading up the group. The other men were driving Saint Mary's Mission's cattle behind them so that they didn't have to eat the dust if there was any.

"So, Dead Rabbits," Immanuel said, "I don't get it?"

"The Gaelic for the words, dead rabbit," Vallon

said, then said, "Conini marbh. Well, the word rabbit is a phonetic corruption of the word *raibead*, which means big hulking person, man to be feared, so Dead Raibead would mean a man to be greatly feared, understand?"

"No, I do not understand," Immanuel said.

"Me neither," Uzziah joined in.

"Ya have to grow up in Ireland and speak the Gaelic to get it, but trust me, it doesn't mean simply *Dead Rabbit*, that would be stupid."

It took them several days to get to the Alder Gulch area. The whole place couldn't be more than fifty people, and they were living in shacks or tents. When they came into the area, everyone doing placer mining looked up from the creek, and some followed them onto the shop, which was also a tent, where Con Kohrs slaughtered the beef that he sold to the miners. No one at that time was interested in anything but steaks. Boiling beef and any other such concoction of beef dishes was totally rejected. If it wasn't a steak, then they didn't want it.

Con walked out. He was a youngish man, well built, and not tall, but not short. His shoulders showed the world what he'd been doing–hanging and butchering cattle. He had a beard like most of the men of the era, and his attire was nearly atrocious.

"Whatcha doin' chere?" he asked Vallon.

"Gonna sell ya these beeves," Vallon said.

"But it ain't the time fer that now," Con said, taking a wider stance as if that was enough to back up his words.

"Well, I'm gonna go outta the rustling business, and I thought maybe it'll be more cost-effective ifn ya was to get into the raisin' beef business," Vallon said, indicating the herd which was grazing easily up the Blacktail Creek Valley.

"I'm a butcher, not a cattleman," Con said, still looking at the herd.

"Well, a couple of the boys would stay with cha and getcha used to 'em. It ain't that hard and think of the increase in yer profit, eh?" Vallon said.

"Let's go down to the saloon," Con said.

Vallon signaled Immanuel and Uzziah to follow him down to the saloon, which was a giant tent with tables and chairs in it, and a plank bar set between two barrels of whiskey.

Buck had heard the word *whiskey* and was right alongside them. Both partners looked over, but no one said anything. After all, he was the one who had basically turned this whole deal.

"I stay watch horses," Abooksigun said.

"Good idea," Uzziah said as the four men walked into the saloon.

The crowd, well, there were ten people, about, they were sitting around at different tables, and drinking whiskey. There was one man who had a warm beer.

"The whiskey's cold and the beer's warm," Con said as he took a big round table.

Immanuel noticed that Con had on a pistola over his butcher's apron, and it looked from the blood that was splattered on the apron and gun, that the gun was worn whenever the apron was.

"Give a bottle and how many glasses, anybody want beer?" Con asked.

No one said anything about wanting beer.

"Bottle and five glasses, then," he said to the barkeep.

The barkeep was old, really old. Looked like he might have fought in the Revolutionary War or certainly the War of 1812. As he brought the glasses and the bottle over, he set the bottle on the table and took the five shot glasses from a greasy pocket in his apron.

"How old are ya, pops?" Immanuel asked. Uzziah just looked at his partner, whom he considered less than sociable.

The old man looked at Immanuel and then all around the table, set the glasses around in front of everyone, and started to walk off.

"Yer age, old timer?" Immanuel asked as he grabbed the barkeep by the arm.

For an older man, the barkeep moved swiftly. He pulled the pistola, cocked it, and set it alongside Immanuel's temple. "Old enough to put a winder in yer head," the old man said in a raspy voice.

Immanuel let go and the old man walked away, keeping an eye on Immanuel as he did so.

"Don't mind him," Con said. "Wandered in a year ago and nobody knows nothin' 'bout 'im, best to let it go, I say," Con said as he poured shots all around.

"Thank ye," Buck said and downed the shot before everyone else was even served.

"Now, there's a thirsty man," Con said and poured Buck another drink.

They sat there and sipped, well, Buck tried to sip, then finally walked to the bar and ordered a beer chaser from the old man. They seemed to have a normal conversation, then Buck came back, sipping on the warm beer.

"How much?" Con finally asked.

"Going price," Vallon said.

"I ain't got no $20 a steer," Con said. "I'll give ya $10 a piece, but ya hafta take gold and silver."

"Done," Vallon said, and the two men shook hands.

When they went back out to the hitching post, Abooksigun was still sitting his pony and his head was on a swivel. Buck had bought a bottle from the old man and handed it to Abooksigun.

"What I do with this?" the Injun asked Buck.

"Keep it fer me, and only give it to me after supper," Buck said as he mounted back up.

Vallon had already appointed the men who wanted to stay. There were several of them who wanted to stake claims and try their hand at placer mining, and when they weren't mining, they would handle the steers for Con.

As they got back on the road and headed for the next range of mountains on their way back to the Little Bighorn and the Yellowstone, Immanuel rode up alongside Buck. Buck looked at him funny, then stared straight ahead.

"The old man..." Immanuel said, trailing off.

"What 'bout 'im?" Buck asked.

"Ya had yerself a near two-minute conversatin' with 'im," Immanuel said.

"Yeah, he was right friendly."

"Who was he?" Immanuel asked.

"Jules Beni," Buck said.

"He just came out and told ya that?"

"That's how I knows," Buck said. "A man like that don't wanna be touched by no strangers."

"What's he doin' down thisaway?" Immanuel asked.

"Guess he's takin' a break from robbin' stagecoaches in the Colorado territory," Buck offered.

"He told ya that, too?!"

"Nah, I done heard 'bout him when I was in Texas, he's a bad hombre, yer lucky it was a good day fer him, otherwise it woulda been a bad day fer ya," Buck said and rode his horse up to where his bottle resided, alongside Abooksigun.

"What was that all 'bout?" Uzziah had ridden up and asked his partner.

"Bunch a lies. I swear that man can throw 'em out there," Immanuel said, his face a mask of annoyance.

"What'd he say?"

"Nothin' worth listenin' to," Immanuel said.

8

They decided that since the women and children were with them, and they had gotten rid of the herd, they would travel a bit more north-by-northeast. This would take them into Blackfeet territory, but with the extra guns and all, it was a fairly safe bet. All in all, with the few men they'd left at Alder Gulch, they had about thirty-five wranglers, nearly all Irish, and men who had fought in the street fights of New York City. Wily men who knew their way around guns, knives, and hand-to-hand fighting. Not to mention the women, who were equally as tough.

About three weeks after leaving Alder Gulch and halfway back to Wolf Point, there came a scream from one of the wagons of women. Immanuel, Uzziah, and Vallon all rode over there to see what the problem was.

"These little bastards got themselves some teeths now!" the wet nurse said as she stuck her head from the wagon. "I am done feedin' 'em."

Immanuel tied Stygian to the back of the wagon and climbed in, "I'll take care of it, don't worry," he said.

The two pups were good-sized now, and they could see. They were busy exploring the wagon and treating all the children to their licks and playful bites.

"Anybody got any cheesecloth?" he asked the ladies in the back of the wagon.

"Here's some I used to use to cover my barrel when I was making cheese," an older woman said and handed it to Immanuel.

"Why don't she just use my bubbly pot?" one woman asked, and she produced something that looked like a pitcher, but at the end of the spout, it had a vulcanized top with small holes in it.

"That's a great idea," Immanuel said.

"And ya've had this all along, have ya? Even when I was sufferin' with their early teeth!?!" the wet nurse asked.

"Ya didn't ask. Besides, thought ya was having a veritable spasm when ya was feedin' 'em," she said, and all the other women laughed.

"Ya bitch!" the wet nurse said and grabbed the insulting woman and they began to fight.

Uzziah and Abooksigun were riding behind the wagon with the Irish Wolfhound pups in it, and then all of a sudden, two women tumbled from the wagon. They were going at it tooth and nail, scratching, biting, and screaming.

Immanuel stuck his head out from between the partition of the wagon canvas. "Don't hurt her teats!" he yelled, and that got all the Irish cowhands laughing.

Finally, Immanuel jumped from the moving wagon, lost his footing, and went down in the middle of the catfight.

"Hey! Hey!" he screamed as their bites and tears

with their long nails were getting at him as much as they were at each other.

Uzziah jumped down off Shadow and separated the two women who continued to swing at each other.

"Don't bruise her teats!" Immanuel yelled again as he stood and tried to put himself back together.

Luckily, the bubbly pot was not harmed, and the wet nurse, it was decided, would ride in the other wagon where she had not made enemies.

"Y'all hafta pay me for the bubbly pot," the owner of the pot said as she extended her hand.

"How much?"

She whispered a price in Immanuel's ear.

"That's highway robbery!" he shouted, and she grabbed the pot away from him. "Okay, okay, okay!" Immanuel said and got the coins from his purse.

They got back to riding after everyone had had a much-needed break.

"Ya owe me," Immanuel said to Uzziah as he held out his hand.

"What fer?"

"Half the bubbly pot, now!" Immanuel said, and as Uzziah was digging in his vest, Abooksigun spoke up.

"Trouble on the crests," he said, and they all looked and saw Injuns sitting on the horizon line of a hill up ahead.

The entire party had stopped at this time, and all the men were checking their weapons and getting ready for what they thought might be a terrific fight. Vallon was hollering out orders in Gaelic, and God knew what he was saying, but none of the three friends did.

"Tell them wait," Abooksigun said, and kicked his pony up and was gone from the trio, just like that.

As he rode toward the hill which led to the horizon crest, the other Injuns just sat their ponies, not moving at all.

"Whatcha suppose he's gonna do?" Immanuel asked Uzziah.

"Broker a peace, start a war—yer guess is as good as mine."

They watched him ride his pony up the hill, and they admired the way he sat his horse. Abooksigun had saved them back in Virginia, and he was known by Uzziah's ma and pa. Rahab had even drawn his likeness. Uzziah said a silent prayer that no harm would come to their good friend.

"What the hell's goin' on?" Vallon asked. "Are we in fer it?"

Immanuel looked at the son of the Irish leader who had been killed on the streets of New York. In some ways, they were different. Immanuel had been the son of an explorer, and his mother, a Mandan, had raised him like he was full-blooded, but he wasn't. He had seen tragedy early on when it looked as if the Sioux would wipe out his family, and he had risen to the occasion and saved the day. He wondered what it felt like to be the son of an Irish gang leader in New York, and to watch as the man who headed up the other gang, stuck two knives into his pa, and then, watching the two grown leaders talking, perhaps he had even heard the words, then to see the third stab which ensured Priest Vallon's death, and then be right there when his pa died, and to carry the very knife which had ended his pa's life.

There was a way in which it didn't matter that the one thing had happened in the wilderness of the west and the other in the wilderness of the big city. In many ways, they were the same. Neither place cared whether you lived or died, neither place held life in high esteem. Each, the wilderness and the slums of great cities, were breeding grounds for indifference and brutality. Truly, he and Amsterdam Vallon had more in common than he had first supposed.

"We're not sure, Abooksigun wouldn't have ridden up there without knowing something that was not obvious to us. Neither of us recognize the manner of dress or the way they wear their hair. At first, I thought they was Blackfoot, but Uzziah don't think so. Wait, here he comes now," Immanuel said as all three of the leaders looked up and Abooksigun rode right in front of them and whoaed his pony.

"We follow," was all the Algonquin said as he turned his horse and watched the band of twenty-some braves ride down the hill and start through a gap in the hills.

Immanuel and Uzziah kicked their horses up and Vallon rode up alongside Uzziah.

"Is this a good idea?" Vallon asked.

"It beats a lot of others," Uzziah remarked, not taking his eyes off the Injuns up front.

"Who is they?" Immanuel asked Abooksigun.

"They Big Bellies."

"Never heard of 'em," Immanuel said.

"You sure?"

"Course, ain't never heard of no big bellies."

"Also, Gros Ventre."

"I heard of 'em."

"They wait for you," Abooksigun said.

"They's waitin' fer Immanuel?" Uzziah was listening, and now he was getting involved in the conversation.

"Hold up ceremony."

"What ceremony?" Immanuel asked.

"You dance," was all Abooksigun would say.

They followed the Gros Ventre into their village, which was a couple miles away and next to a nice flowing stream. Some of the men wore bowlers and cowboy hats, but all who did also had feathers sticking up out of the hats. The teepees were like most, lodgepole pines set together at their tops with buffalo hides stretched over them. Smoke was roiling from most of the teepees, and when the band of braves was spotted, all the dogs came out with the children, and the children screamed, and the dogs kept barking.

"Quite a welcome!" Vallon said, and Immanuel wondered if Vallon was familiar with the nationality of the Injun, no matter what the tribe. Welcome you for lunch and kill you after supper.

The horses were dismounted and young boys took their war bridles and led them away toward the river, where a herd of other horses were grazing and drinking.

The one Gros Ventre who happened to be, or rather, seemed to be in charge, walked to a teepee and, pulling back the flap, went inside. In a few moments, he was out and motioning for them to enter. Once Abooksigun and Immanuel had entered, he held up his hand, not allowing anyone else in.

Immanuel hadn't seen any Gros Ventre women so far, and as always, he was looking forward to doing just that. His eye for the women had not diminished, and he reckoned that it would never be so. In the dim firelight, they sat in a circle with the leader of the band of braves, and across from them sat what must have been a chief. He had on a cavalry officer's hat all fancied up with beads, feathers, and other trappings. A pipe was presented to them, and Immanuel wondered if he were about to take another spontaneous trip thanks to the peyote buttons, but when he drew on it, it was nothing but tobacco. He was relieved actually.

The *chief* started talking, and sitting next to him was what must have been a medicine man because he was wearing the big buffalo headdress, and every time the chief said certain things, he would nod in agreement.

Both Abooksigun and Immanuel listened, and Immanuel imagined that Abooksigun was like him, not understanding a damned thing. Then Abooksigun spoke up, and Immanuel realized that the Injuns, the Gros Ventre, and his Algonquin friend were speaking close to the same language.

When the conversation came to an almost standstill, Immanuel interjected.

"You speak Gros Ventre?"

"Later," was all Abooksigun said, and the conversation continued for quite some time. Toward the end, it was Abooksigun's turn to speak long, and he did so. When he finished, the chief and certainly the medicine man seemed quite pleased. Then they left the teepee and walked out into the blazing sunlight.

"What's goin' on?" Immanuel asked Abooksigun.

"Later," the Algonquin said, and they, those not in wagons, were led to teepees that had, since their arrival, been prepared for them. Each one had luscious buffalo robes spread where a person could sleep, and a woman was sitting in there and preparing lunch. It sure smelled good.

Vallon, Immanuel, Uzziah, and Abooksigun were put in one teepee, and the rest were spread out.

It was suppertime, so they sat and bowls of a delicious stew were served to them. Probably rabbit, but maybe a little venison was also thrown in, and plenty of greens which had been gathered from around where they lived.

The woman who had prepared it passed Immanuel up and gave bowls to all the others.

"Hey, darlin', ya skipped me," Immanuel protested.

"You no eat," Abooksigun said as he dug in.

"To what do we owe this great hospitality?" Vallon asked anyone who knew the answer.

"Him," Abooksigun said, pointing with his wooden spoon toward Immanuel.

"Well, thanks, Immanuel, had no idea ya guys was known all over the territory," Vallon said.

"We ain't. Come on, Abooksigun, there's something ya ain't tellin' us," Uzziah said.

"Tomorrow he dance for us."

"He, who?" Immanuel asked.

"He, you."

"What?"

"Show me yer chest," Abooksigun said to Immanuel.

"Is this like show me yer tits?" Immanuel said as he unfastened his deerskin shirt and showed his hairy chest.

"Good," Abooksigun said.

"Glad ya approve. Yer not gonna ask me fer a kiss now, are ya?" Immanuel said, pulling his shirt back together.

Abooksigun chuckled and kept right on eating.

"Abooksigun?" Uzziah inquired, not taking his eye off their Algonquin friend.

"Blood Sun Dance tomorrow," Abooksigun whispered.

They had no sooner finished their meal than the medicine man with the big buffalo headdress came in and motioned for Immanuel to follow him.

"This ain't right," Immanuel said, pleading with his partner.

"Old son, I understand, but what can we do?" Uzziah asked.

"Leave!" Immanuel said forcibly.

"You make vow, now must sacrifice," Abooksigun said.

"What vow? Am I gettin' married?" he asked, his spirit rising.

"No, now go, will know later," Abooksigun said, and started back in on his second bowl of stew.

The medicine man took Immanuel to the medicine lodge, which was a structure that was half underground and half above. That symbolized the meeting of heaven and earth to the Gros Ventre. The top was covered with sticks and mud, and when he was led in there, there were others lying about. At first, Immanuel thought that they must be sick because they were lying still and having dots and lines drawn on their arms and legs. One brave was having the moon symbol painted on his forehead, and the others were being completely covered with white paint from head to toe, except where the dots, lines and moon were drawn.

Immanuel knew better than to question what was going on. These Gros Ventre had decided that he had some medicine or that he was something that would help their tribe, so he was going through this ceremony to basically save the others from being killed. He lay down and the painting began. He was tired and went to sleep. The brushstrokes on his body were mesmerizing, and when he awakened, he was being sat up and a crown of sage was being put on his head.

The only thing he could think about then was the crown of thorns which had been placed on Jesus's head while the Roman soldiers scourged him. He certainly hoped that there wasn't going to be any of that going on. They attached similar bands of sage around his ankles and wrists. This all seemed rather innocuous, and he slept until the hours right before sunup.

9

He was awakened with a sharp pain in his chest. When he tried to sit up, he was held down by strong arms, and when he looked by raising up his head, he saw that two cuts had been made in his chest right above the nipples, and that they were now inserting sticks into the cuts, which stuck out on either side.

He was stood up, and there in the medicine lodge were Vallon, Uzziah, Abooksigun, the woman who had fed her milk to the Irish Wolfhounds, and several others of their Irish party. They looked on with trepidation as rawhide ropes were picked up from where they were hung in from the medicine lodge central pole, and the ends of two of these were attached to the sticks, which had blood droplets dripping off them from where he'd been cut.

Someone started drumming, and all the dancers who were thus arrayed started moving in a circle and helped to push out as far as they could with the rawhide throngs pulling on their breast cuts. They hurt like hell!

By noon, the inside of the medicine lodge was sweltering. Sweat was pouring down Immanuel's chest and onto his legs. He only had on a breechcloth, and the memory of how he had been taken out of his clothes escaped him.

He was thirsty, hungry, and the pain in his chest just kept getting worse. He hadn't felt such pains since he'd had the heart attack on board the paddle wheeler, and it was then that he realized the vow which he was sacrificing for was the vow of their partnership. It didn't matter what the Injuns thought he was doing, he was literally dancing in pain in front of the man he had betrayed, reasserting his love and friendship and the fact that he would stay with this one man for the rest of his life, if in fact, he did not die in this god-forsaken ceremony.

This went on for? Well, he kept seeing Uzziah and Abooksigun, but the others had left, evidently in disgust, and not returned. But his two friends remained. Was he there a day, two days, some of those who had been dancing had grown tired of doing so and leaned back against their rawhide straps, and tore the skin from their chests. They had cried out in what—ecstasy or was it sheer pain? He was not going to do that. Surely those who drummed would eventually become tired of the nonstop beating of the skins, and the damned dance would come to a halt.

Then, on the morning of the fourth day, as he was dancing, shuffling his feet to the beat of the music, he tripped and started to fall, but he was connected to the medicine pole, and as he almost hit the ground, he was jerked back to his feet by the rawhide straps that suspended him over heaven and hell itself.

Then, he wasn't there.

He awoke in the spare bedroom that the good doctor in New Orleans had given him, and beside him was the naked body of a woman. Had he slept with his stepmother? A feeling of revulsion overcame him, and he was about to vomit when the young woman turned and looked at him. He gagged down the bile-ridden juices which had almost escaped from his mouth. It was his host's granddaughter, the one who had helped him from the boat. She smiled and caressed his face, and he drew her to him.

She kept saying the most amazing things in French, or he imagined they were amazing because she was speaking so rapidly and the tone of her voice was sweet and lovely, that he almost fell asleep again, until the girl kissed him deeply, her tongue explored the inner regions of his mouth, and both their tongues were like otters playing in a stream, and the sweet, sweet taste of her, and the moistness between her legs.

She reached down and drew him into her. It was heaven. So tight, so moist, so sweet smelling, and as they gyrated together, never losing the taste of the kiss, never letting their mouths part as they coupled there in her grandfather's house. There was no shame, no feeling that he was doing anything wrong. Then her face left his and she licked down to his nipple, bit it off, and spat it on the floor, where it bounced and rolled into a corner!

He screamed, and the medicine lodge sprang back into existence as the second rawhide thong tore loose and he was caught by kind hands.

Uzziah and Abooksigun were there, and Uzziah held a gourd with water which, when he drank it, tasted just like the French girl's mouth. How was that possible?

Abooksigun was singing a song in Algonquin, and it was lovely and sweet, and when Immanuel closed his eyes, he was sure the doctor's granddaughter was there singing her French, the language of love, into his starving ears.

Immanuel left the medicine place and walked down to the river. It was still early in the afternoon. Some of the others who had been in the Blood Sun Dance were down at the stream washing the paint off their bodies. He joined them. They smiled at him, and he smiled back, certain that they had gone through something which only a few had ever been through.

As he stepped into the coolish water that ran over him, he had the feeling that perhaps he would never be the same again. But what did that mean? As he was thinking that, a young Gros Ventre walked through the waters, and before Immanuel could resist, or even think about what the young brave was doing, they were hugging, and the young man's tears felt warm on his naked shoulders, and he, too, wept.

When they parted, the two men, one young and from another tribe and the other older and from the Mandans, looked right into each other's souls and went their separate ways. Immanuel knew that when he crossed over in death that brave would be waiting for him, or he would be waiting when that particular brave crossed over. He was at peace.

As he walked from the stream, he saw the woman

who had nursed the pups. She was walking, and the pups were tumbling and playing with each other as she walked along. He imagined that they had bonded with her. She bent over to play with them and her loose blouse showed her drooping and milk-filled breasts as they dangled from her chest. He had an odd feeling. It didn't have anything to do with having the woman or anything like that. It was a feeling that, for the first time ever in his life, he saw the female breast for what it was —a life-giving tool. He would never see another breast without feeling this way, and that, in itself, was a part of the change that was going through him at this moment.

The wind was coming from the south, and the breeze bent the willows which grew near the banks of the stream, and the way their branches reached out and caught each other, and then fell back, the way the skirt on the milkmaid—that's how he thought of her now—flew out, and came back, it was all a part of the rhythm of things. Everything was connected, everything was a part of everything else, and it wasn't a thought, it was a sensation which emanated from the bottom of his heart.

Then, he thought about his heart, how he had worried about it, lying awake at night after Uzziah was sound asleep and he was struggling with the thought that it just might give out on him, and he would die alone without anyone nearby, well, anyone nearby who wasn't sleeping. He wasn't worried about that now. His heart would run till it ran no more, much like a wounded deer. Perhaps his heart had been wounded, and these were the last few hundred yards of its running, but did it really matter?

Uzziah and Abooksigun were coming from the medicine lodge and they were deep in conversation. He loved those two men, and his heart went out to them, and he wondered what they could be talking about, but that, too, didn't matter.

Uzziah looked down to where Immanuel was wiping the water from the stream off his naked body.

"They tell me something," Abooksigun said.

"Who told you?"

"Big medicine man. Those who do Blood Sun close to end."

"End?"

"Whatever that mean," Abooksigun said.

"Let's not say anything 'bout that, okay?" Uzziah suggested.

"We all close to end. Everything see will die!" he said and made a broad stroke with his arm, which included the birds in the trees, the trees themselves, the river, those around the river. And Immanuel himself.

That night, after Uzziah had placed the poultices on the wounds on Immanuel's chest and cooked a supper which he knew Immanuel liked, well, liked was too subtle. The man ate the deer steak as if he were breathing. The potatoes which the Gros Ventre had grown were boiled and mashed. Uzziah added bacon grease to them and made gravy from the frying of the steaks in the big pan.

In both Dutch ovens, he had johnnycakes and biscuits, and he steamed the edible greens—oxeye daisy, sweet root, and Shepherd's purse—when the steaks were finishing up. All in all, Vallon, Buck, Abooksigun, Immanuel, the woman who had fed the pups—they finally heard her name, Valerie—and Uzziah sat there and finished off every single bite. There were, naturally, scraps which had been fed to the pups who were getting bigger with every single day.

Uzziah wanted to cook for the entire clan, but there were resources and then there were resources. The others ate well, cooking their own meals over separate fires, and the laughter that sprang up from time to time gladdened everyone's heart, especially Immanuel's.

"You, okay?" Uzziah asked his partner of so many years.

"Never better."

"Your chest?"

"Filled."

"I mean the wounds?"

"Healed."

"What was that all about anyways?" Uzziah wondered, and he wasn't the only one.

"In heaven's name, I have no idea."

"I know," Abooksigun said, having eavesdropped.

"Oh yeah, fill us in," Uzziah said.

"Bad things were in our hearts," Abooksigun said, and all three of them thought how they had almost stampeded a herd into these loving folks, "But fool save us," Abooksigun added, and they knew he was referring to Buck who, for want of whiskey, had gone into the lions' den, then invited them all in, "Fool's honor important. The Gros Ventre medicine man visited by dreams of us, especially you, weak heart," Abooksigun said, looking at Immanuel, "but weak heart no longer, yes?"

"Yes," Immanuel said, and he stood up and addressed all the campfires and all the suppers which were winding down. "I'd like to propose a toast," he said as he raised his coffee mug, and everyone scrambled to pour a dram of whiskey into quickly emptied mugs. Uzziah offered Immanuel a shot, but he slowly shook his head, then spoke the toast. "To Buck *Keith* Krieter" —and you could see Buck bow up at the mention of the name he did not like—"a man who goes 'bout his business havin' no idea how the Lord God Almighty is usin' him for the good of us all, To Buck!" Immanuel shouted, and the whole crew broke into an Irish song of praise.

"Be thou my vision, O Lord of my heart.
Naught be all else to me, save that
Thou art.
Thou my best thought, by day or by
night,
Waking or sleeping, Thy presence my
light."

When that verse had ended, Vallon stepped forward and sang the second verse as a solo.

Be Thou my wisdom, and Thou my true
word.
I ever with Thee and Thou with me,
Lord,
Thou my great Father, and I Thy
true son.
Thou in me dwelling and I with Thee
one."

Then the whole group of the Irish stood and raised such a swelling of song that Buck began to weep, and as he wept, Immanuel went to him and put his arm around his shoulder.

"Riches I heed not, nor vain, empty
praise,
Thou mine inheritance, now and
always.
Thou and Thou only first in my heart,
"igh King of Heaven, my treasure Thou
art."

Then everyone stood and finished the Irish hymn of praise. Even Buck joined in, who knew that he could belt out a song?

"High King of Heaven, my victory won,
May I reach Heaven's joys, O bright
Heaven's sun.
Heart of my own heart, whatever befall,
Still be my vision, O Ruler of all.
Heart of my own heart, whatever befall,
Still be my vision, O Ruler of all."

10

The rest of the journey to Wolf Point was uneventful, if you can call the harmony with which these travelers went their own way uneventful. The Blackfeet were seen at one point, and even though the Gros Ventre were part of that tribal affiliation, they had not heard of their passing, but when one of the members of the Blackfeet braves recognized Immanuel, who seemed to be riding Stygian under a spell of peace and grace, as he rode right toward the party. Uzziah could see them conversing in sign, Immanuel was very good at it, and finally they yelped some, and Immanuel rode back.

"What was that all about?" Uzziah asked.

"They are gettin' the hang of the cattle business. They've even got a few calves which, hopefully, will weather the storms to come. They are very grateful and say that no one at Wolf Point need worry 'bout them, unless someone acts agin 'em."

So, thought Uzziah, then it was settled, at least for now. He knew that the Blackfeet would have a short memory once their herd had dwindled, chiefs had changed places, and another winter had come and gone, but it looked very much like this winter things would be okay. When the old chief died or when there was not enough for their growing people, then trouble would most likely raise its ugly head.

But as Immanuel and Uzziah spied the clouds in the east building and coming their way, Abooksigun also saw them, the three men tried to encourage the rest of the group to get out of slow motion and start traveling a bit faster. The Irishmen had been through a couple of winters in the Big Hole and were not impressed by the gathering clouds.

"So, it'll snow, so what?" Vallon said.

"Out here, in these prairies, it can blow and snow at the same time. If that happens, we'll have to be camped, otherwise, we'll lose each other's tracks and end up snow blind and stranded," Uzziah tried to point out.

"So, let's find a good camp and hunker down," Vallon suggested.

There was a butte, a couple of them, up ahead, so they headed in that direction. Immanuel figured if they got on the leeward side of the butte, the storm's ferocity would be decreased, and they could weather it better. Vallon, his wagons, and his Irishmen followed along. As always, things spied on horizons can sometimes be a lot further than you think. By the time they got there, the snow was blowing from behind, the horses liked that, and they could barely see the wagons and the other men.

There was a stream flowing toward the Missouri, Immanuel imagined, and he took all the lariats he had, tied them between the Irish wagons and the rope corral where they were going to put the horses. If it got bad enough, the ropes would be the only things that saved them. The wind was howling when Uzziah stuck his head into the wagons.

"Ladies, boys, and girls, if you git out of the wagon to do any private business, please 'member to hold on to the ropes that my partner had tied between the wagons and the corral. We's backed up against these two buttes, and the winds will come from 'round the butte, but they will not be as fierce as the wind directly from the storm. We got water, and I will try to fix some foods, if the weather allows me, otherwise, jerked meat, water, and old biscuits will do the trick till we's can dig out from what I think will be a terrific storm."

He made basically the same speech in both wagons, then got back to where Immanuel and Abooksigun had tied tarps around the bases of several mesquite bushes and pulled them so that the snow wouldn't be falling on them. The place where they'd done that was close to the rising base of the butte and offered some protection. They had an oil lamp that Uzziah was going to try to cook by. The clouds and the flying snow had pretty much obliterated the sun and it was dark way before sunset.

Uzziah managed several Dutch-oven-fulls of beans and bacon, and holding onto the rope, he struggled around to the wagons and dished out beans and bacon to most of them. He'd actually given so much away to the Irish that when he got back to the lean-to, there was barely any in the bottom of both the Dutch ovens. Abooksigun, Immanuel, and Uzziah scraped the bottom of both ovens with day-old biscuits and settled in for the storm.

Uzziah settled in and, looking at both his companions, realized there couldn't be better partners to weather this storm with. It got so that by the time the sun had set, the howling of the wind lulled them to a sleep. They were warm enough, considering the clothes they had on and the buffalo robes they hunkered down under.

About halfway through the night, they were awakened by screams. Uzziah, Immanuel, and Abooksigun were up and out of their warm beds. A corner of the lean-to had collapsed and snow had covered the bottom of the Injun's bedroll. He fixed that while the two partners went to see what the matter was.

The screaming was coming from one of the wagons, and when they got there, the milkmaid, as Immanuel was referring to her, was hysterical.

"He's out there! He's out there!" she kept screaming.

She had taken the pups out to pee and do their business, then the male had wandered off, and she couldn't find him. Her nursing them for nearly three weeks had grown an attachment between them which was almost like that of a mother and child.

"You keep the female from gettin' out, we'll find 'im," Immanuel said. The pups weren't small now, well, they were going to be Irish Wolfhounds, the largest of just about any breed of dog.

The wind was still howling, but there were lulls in the wind, and during those lulls, they could hear the crying of the pup.

"He just out there!" Uzziah said, pointing in the direction he believed the crying was coming from, "I'll go out and get him!"

Immanuel grabbed Uzziah. "Young son, you will freeze yer nards off out there, and get lost! Just let 'im be, we got another dog."

"Okay," Uzziah said, and as Immanuel turned to make his way back toward the horses and the lean-to, Uzziah let go of the rope and went in the direction of the crying pup.

Every time there was a lull in the screaming wind, Uzziah used his hearing to bring him, he thought, closer to the pup. Its crying was enough to break his heart, and finally he saw a lump in the snow behind a mesquite bush, and sure enough, that was the male of the two pups. It was shivering and would die of exposure if Uzziah didn't find either his way back to the wagons or some other shelter.

As if God had arranged it, there was a break in the storm, and the moon shone off the side of the butte. Uzziah and the pup he had tucked inside his coat were very close, and he ran, as best he could, toward it just before it disappeared behind the blinding snow and the howling of the wind. He stumbled and fell when he reached the side of the butte, and as he found his way along it, he groped along the ground—looking for what, he wasn't sure—but then his hand disappeared into a hole, and when he explored the hole, it was as big enough for a bear to go through. He decided he would rather die at the hands of a bear than freeze, so he pushed himself and the pup, who was secured under his coat, inside the hole.

Uzziah took out a match and lit it. The hole turned

out to be a good-sized cave with a narrow entrance. He got further back in the cave where he could barely hear the wind and the raging storm. He gathered sticks and such from around the cave, and within five minutes, with the help of his lucifers, he had a nice little fire going. He pulled the pup, who was still shivering, and held him close to the fire, and lay down there putting his body warmth around the back of the pup, who was about the size of a badger. With the fire in the front and Uzziah rubbing its body, the pup soon stopped shivering.

"Yer a good boy, Straggler, good boy. Good ole boy, Straggler," Uzziah said, rubbing the puppy, and then he realized the male of the two had been named. He was Straggler, or Strag. Perfect. Soon, with all the sweet talk from Uzziah and the rubbing, Straggler was asleep, and so was Uzziah.

"We gots to find 'em, we gots to!" Immanuel said to Abooksigun.

"Stay, he warrior. Stay," was all Abooksigun said, and unfortunately, Immanuel knew that the Injun was right. If he went out and tried to find Uzziah and the pup, he, too, would be lost.

"Damned Uzziah!" Immanuel cursed.

"Blessed Uzziah," Abooksigun whispered, and Immanuel realized he was right, if anything, a blessing should be sent out to his partner, not a curse! He lay there trying to think of how he could possibly save Uzziah, and then he awoke. He was sure he'd heard a shot, or maybe two, couldn't tell the way the wind was blowing. Was Uzziah signaling him for help? He went back to sleep, exhausted at the very thought of it.

The fire had almost gone out when the bear—thankfully, it was not a grizzly—had found the cave. He pushed through the snow to get inside and was surprised when he saw the dwindling fire.

He made his way toward the fire and smelled a warm puppy. Dinner! He rushed forward, growling.

Uzziah awakened when he heard the growls and, rolling away from the fire, shot his revolver, which he had just traded for at the Gros Ventre village. He hadn't even had time to try it out, but it fired, and fired and fired, until the hammer came down on an empty shell. Every shot had hit the bear, and some were in the face.

Then, Uzziah heard the sound of a different growling, and looking down in front of the bear was Straggler, bowed up in a fierce pose, and growling ferociously. Uzziah had no idea a pup could growl like that!

The bear was looking all over in front of him, trying to find the wolf that was growling at him. Uzziah ran toward the bear, and when Uzziah swatted Straggler out of the way, he yelped when he hit the side of the cave, but at least for now, he was out of harm's way.

The bear grabbed at Uzziah, trying to pick him up in a bear hug, but Uzziah had always been fast for a heavy man. He ducked and swirled under the bear's closing grasp and jumped on the bear's back. The bear's growl filled the cave, and he tried to stand up all the way, but the ceiling was low.

Meantime, Uzziah had pulled his Bowie knife out

and was stabbing the bear in the chest, the neck, and wherever else he could. He just kept stabbing, knowing that eventually the bear was going to shake him off, and if he was lucky, his death would be quick.

The bear's paws kept coming back and raking themselves on Uzziah's arm, which had more or less locked around the bear's neck. Stab, stab, stab, stab, then with a great shaking of his body, Uzziah went flying off the bear's back and hit the side of the cave. He yelped just as Straggler had done, and seeing that his tormentor was off, the bear, crouching low, came running at Uzziah. It was over, but then something darted between the bear's legs, and thank the Lord, the bear was a male! Straggler took hold of the bear's testicles and bit down hard.

The shriek which came from the bear filled the cave, but every time he reached to get Straggler off his balls, the hanging things with Straggler attached swung back and away from his grasp.

Uzziah looked around quickly. There sat the Hawken. He picked it up and fired, but the powder had become wet, and the hammer clicked down on nothingness. He still had the Bowie, and as he ran toward the bear, it was so busy looking for what was biting him that he had his head down and was searching.

Uzziah pulled the knife up to its greatest height, hitting the top of the cave when he did so, his hands smarting like hell, and just then, he remembered Ophelia's plunging of the knife into her rapist's heart, and jumping up as best he could, he brought the long knife down on the bear's neck.

The bear stood up and threw Uzziah off him, but the look on his face was confusing to Uzziah. He roared once again, but when he tried to move, he collapsed, the air whooshing out of him.

Straggler started yelping like nobody's business, he was caught beneath the bear's weight.

In what he later thought could only be a feat of herculean strength, Uzziah grabbed the bear's head and twisted him off Straggler, who ran to Uzziah as fast as he could!

"It's okay, big brown wanted to eat us. We showed him, though, that last trick of yourn was special, real fightin' hound dog stuff!" Uzziah whispered to the pup. Uzziah pulled the big brown up behind him, snuggled up to the warm, dead bear, and started the fire up again. The pup rewarded Uzziah by licking his hands until he —the pup—fell back asleep. Uzziah was warm with the bear to his back, and he sure hoped the bear was really dead. Dead, dead!

By the time Uzziah had dug his way through what looked like a couple feet of snow that covered the butte, it was already into the day. He had wanted to drag the bear out so they could feast on it, but when he looked, the wagons had gone, and they were nowhere on this side of the butte. The adventures of the night, and the fact that he and Straggler were both worn out, he'd slept way too late. The pup was chewing on part of the bear, good dog, and after they'd made it from the cave, they stood there, and it looked very much like they had been written off as missing in action.

Uzziah immediately went up the butte to a point where he could look out on the plains. He wished he had Immanuel's binocs, but fairly soon, he saw something that looked like it was moving away from the butte.

He had the Hawken with him and fired a shot into the air, then started reloading it.

Immanuel, Abooksigun, and Vallon had searched for hours that morning, but it looked like the mountain man and the pup had disappeared into thin air. Neither of them was anywhere to be seen. Immanuel would not give up, he circled the butte once, and still nothing!

"We'd better not tarry," Vallon said, looking off toward the west where it looked very much as if another storm front was headed their way.

Immanuel turned to Abooksigun to see what the Algonquin would say. All Abooksigun could do was shrug as he looked toward the new stormfront that was coming their way.

They had taken off, hoping to at least get closer to the pastures along the Missouri. Immanuel was devastated. He kept looking behind him, and seeing the same thing, nothing.

It was then he heard a shot, and it was a Hawken. He'd heard enough of those shots to know it was a Hawken. He heard some struggling at the back of one of the wagons, and when he rode around in that direction, Shadow broke his reins loose from where they were tied up and was running back toward the butte.

Then another Hawken shot resounded over the plains, sounding like the thunder that might be coming at them from the new storm.

"That's him!" Immanuel shouted and turned Stygian right around and headed back.

Vallon threw up his arms as if to say, *We have to get ahead of the next storm*!

When Stygian caught up with Shadow, Immanuel swore the horse was smiling. Of course that was crazy. Horses don't smile, do they?

"Let's go git 'im, boy, let's go git 'im!" Immanuel shouted over to Shadow, and he kicked Stygian into a higher gear. The two horses were running neck and neck when they saw the lumpy form standing at the base of the butte, and getting closer, Immanuel could see the other pup, whose name he did not know yet, tucked into Uzziah's coat.

Uzziah couldn't get up on Shadow by himself, and Immanuel saw that his left arm was dangling a bit.

"What happened to ya?" Immanuel said, dismounting and running to him.

"This pup," Uzziah began. "This pup..." He began again, but the tears came to his eyes as Immanuel took it all in.

11

The big storm behind them petered out over the plains, and the next few days, the story of Straggler made its way around the wagons, and all the Irish could do was brag that he was how he was because he was an *Irish* Wolfhound.

When they pulled into the ranch, things looked pretty much the same, except that the place was covered with a patina of snow. Father De Smet came running out from the two mountain men's cabin, joyous and singing God's praises for letting everyone get back safely.

When it was explained to the good padre that those Irish who had come back with them were the rustlers who had taken the cattle from St. Mary's Mission, he was aghast until he was introduced to Amsterdam Vallon.

"We've met, and I knew yer father," De Smet said to Amsterdam.

"Yer lyin'," Amsterdam said. "But no matter, here's

monies I owes ya," Vallon said as he handed the priest a sheaf of paper money.

De Smet took the money and folded it into his robe, then continued with the conversation. "No, I did know yer father! It was shortly before the big fight at Five Points, and I don't know if you know this, but I gave him absolution for everything he'd done, and everything he was about to do," De Smet said.

Amsterdam looked at the priest as if a prayer of his had been answered.

"I thought he'd died outside of grace," Vallon said.

"No, and later, when he was in his coffin, and about to be buried at Green-Wood Cemetery, I gave him the Last Rites—"

"That was ye, old man!?!" Amsterdam shouted and took De Smet into his arms, and the two of them embraced for a long time. "Ye seemed so much bigger, but then again, I was but a boy!" Amsterdam said, then began spouting off in Gaelic, and Father De Smet was praising God in French. No one was sure what was going on.

They built a fire in the chuck wagon so that Father De Smet could hold confessional for all the Irish. This time, there was a line that ran from the chuck to Uzziah and Immanuel's cabin. Those in the back of the line waited inside their cabin to keep warm, and even a bit of brandy, which Amsterdam had brought along, was doled out to those about to confess.

It took the entire day, and when it was over, they had tables brought together in a big circle and a huge fire in the middle, and there was a feast. Uzziah and Buck did most of the cooking, and Buck began to understand how much better of a cook he could be with just a bit more attention to the job and less to the bottle sitting nearby.

Uzziah, Immanuel, Abooksigun, De Smet, and Vallon sat at what could be considered the high part of the round table, and during the meal, Father De Smet turned to Vallon.

"Is it true?" De Smet asked.

"Is what true, padre?" Vallon answered.

"Will you go back to New York and seek revenge on William Poole?"

"I will, Father, I will," Amsterdam said.

"But Jesus would tell you to turn the other cheek," De Smet warned.

"He would, Father, he would, but did God the Father Almighty not tell his son, who had been crucified, that he would make the devil, Satan, himself, a footstool for Jesus?"

"Yer quoting the first verse of the 110th Psalm, when King David said, 'The LORD said unto my Lord, Sit thou at my right hand, until I make thine enemies thy footstool,'" De Smet quoted.

"Aye, and that's exactly what I will do with Bill the Butcher," Vallon said.

"All I can do is counsel against it, my son. Remember, vengeance belongs to God, and God alone."

"But sometimes, God's hands are here on this earth and his work is accomplished thusly," Vallon said.

"Well, that is a fact. If the Roman Centurion had refused to crucify Jesus, where would that have left us?" De Smet said, pouring more whiskey into Vallon's glass.

Uzziah and Immanuel were quieter than usual at this festival of the Irish. Uzziah was surprised that Immanuel had not partaken of the whiskey and had barely had two glasses of wine to wash down the fine meal.

"Are ya all right?" Uzziah whispered to Immanuel.

"I should be askin' ya that question, I'm not the one who single-handedly killed a papa bear."

Straggler was sitting beneath Uzziah's feet as he was feeding him scraps.

"Well, I had some help there, ya know?" Uzziah said, putting the scrap between his legs so that Straggler could gobble it up!

But Immanuel was not to be outdone, he took some venison and brought it under the table for the other pup.

"What ya gonna call her?" Uzziah asked, peeking under the table as the two dogs did not fight over the scraps, but were contentedly eating what they had been offered.

"Her name is Cerberus," Immanuel said, looking down at her.

"The hound of hell? No!" Uzziah protested.

"That's right, hell's hound."

"You're too well read sometimes. Why don't ya just give the dog a dog's name?"

"Like Straggler, that's real nice," Immanuel said.

"Well, he was late comin' back to the wagons."

"Straggler and Cerberus, I like it. They sound like they belong together."

"Can we call her Serb?" Uzziah asked.

"Well, she's my dog, so, I guess."

"They're both our dogs, don't ya think?"

Straggler was up with his front paws on Uzziah's lap, almost pushing the poor man off his chair.

"Well, ya could say that, but don't think it's true. Ya saved Straggler's life, and he ain't ever gonna forgit it."

Winter came in with a vengeance of its own, and Father De Smet had settled in enough at the ranch that he was fine with staying there till spring. The Irish dug into the surrounding hills and had themselves several fine houses that were ready by Christmas. The children had a lot of fun in the snow, building snowmen and having snowball fights.

Abooksigun moved into the mountain men's cabin, and the good Father moved in with Vallon. Both Uzziah and Immanuel figured he would be working on the Irishman all winter in hopes of discouraging him from seeking the revenge he was after. Besides, it had been quite a while, and perhaps sleeping dogs were best left lying?

For Immanuel, it was the first time, ever, that he had felt he was fine without being in the mountains. He didn't even mind the fact that they really lived in a community and everyone was calling it Wolf Point. Well, that was what it was, right?

When the spring came, Father De Smet caught the first paddle wheeler back to Saint Louis, and Vallon went with him. Once again, no one was sure who would have gone without the other one going. Father De Smet never stopped trying to keep Vallon from doing what his soul asked him to do—kill the man who had killed his father.

As the summer wore on, and Uzziah had written his ma and pa and let them know his new address, he also gathered all the old newspapers from the paddle wheeler in exchange for chopping wood.

He was reading one day, out in the sun, outside the cabin. The day was pleasantly warm, and Immanuel was playing with both the Irish Wolfhounds, which had grown by leaps and bounds. They could jump up on you and put their paws on your shoulders. It was fairly ridiculous. Uzziah had known ponies who were smaller.

"Hey, it looks like Amsterdam done what he said he was gonna do," Uzziah said.

Immanuel left the pups, who followed him over to the table where Uzziah was reading the newspaper.

"Read it to me," Immanuel said.

"Well, it just says that he's the head of the Dead Rabbits. Looks like he's resurrected the gang. Here's the article, it ain't big, just that he's back in New York and leading the Irish again."

Immanuel took the newspaper and started reading.

"It don't say much 'bout old William the Butcher."

"His real name was William Poole," Uzziah remembered.

"Still don't say nothin' 'bout 'im," Immanuel said.

"Yeah, maybe Vallon thought twice 'bout doin' what he was thinkin' 'bout doin', ya know?"

"Maybe, but he don't seem the kind of guy who'd forgit when it came to the death of his pa."

The days went on like that. The Irish ran the place fairly well, and Jack Tate learned to get along with them. They didn't own any of the cows, but most of them had worked with cows in Ireland and were glad to be back working with livestock.

Jack left the place to get his wife and her sister, the woman whose child had been entrusted to him, and he'd gotten killed. Uzziah and Immanuel had never met the young gunslinger, but he'd died in a poker game when the herd hadn't gone very far. That's all the information they had, and Jack Tate wasn't exactly giving out any more details.

Uzziah got a letter from Rahab, and it was full of all sorts of details about their home in the Shenandoah Valley, and how tensions were riding high concerning the possibility of a civil war starting up. It seemed there was a new president. Abraham Lincoln had beaten out John C. Breckinridge and been installed in the White House. Rahab, Uzziah's mother, seemed to think that the election pointed to a swing toward the war, but nobody was surc.

Immanuel and Uzziah had talks about what would happen if the north and south did fight. What would they do? In the 1860s Virginia, it was more important which state you were from than being a citizen of the United States.

"Whatcha gonna do?" Immanuel asked.

"'Bout what?"

"Ifn, the war does come, stay chere where it won't bother none of us, or go and fight?" Immanuel asked.

"I'll always be a Virginian first, Immanuel, ya know that. And the Shenandoah will be right in the thick of it, and my family, ya know?"

"So, ya'll fight, then?"

"Most likely, yeah."

Well, they would wait and see what the crazy politicians had in mind. Maybe there would be war, and maybe there wouldn't, they'd wait and see.

Jack Tate came back late in the year. His wife was real nice, and lo and behold, the minute his sister-in-law got there, she set her sights on Buck Krieter. They seemed to be just friends at first, then one day, Buck came to their cabin door.

He knocked, which was strange, usually, everyone just hollered out and came on in.

Uzziah went to the door of the cabin. Immanuel was asleep, taking a bit of an afternoon nap.

"What is it, Buck?"

"Molly and I want ya to marry us," Buck said kind of shy-like.

"Really?"

"Yeah, we think it's best," Buck said, then lowered his voice even more. "She's with child," he finished up and looked down at his boots and scratched the earth outside the cabin.

"Well, I'd be glad to, when ya thinkin'?"

"Sooner than later."

EPILOGUE

They held the wedding in the big barn so they could have a dance afterward. Everybody was there, and the Irish had instruments, and the dancing was fine. About halfway through the evening, Uzziah and Immanuel was approached by Abooksigun.

"I go back," the Injun said.

"To the land of vapors?" Immanuel asked.

"Mud pits lie. No, back home."

"To where exactly?" Uzziah wanted to know.

"Whites call New England."

"When?" Immanuel asked.

"Tonight, after party."

"We'll miss ya, ya know that, right?"

"Of course," he said, and then he headed right out on the dance floor and began to dance what they could only imagine to be an Injun leaving dance done to the tune of an Irish jig. Those dancing all stopped and watched with a great deal of appreciation, then when he was through, he shook hands with everyone, bride and groom included, and then went to his pony and rode off.

Uzziah and Immanuel stood there watching their Algonquin friend ride out under the moonlight. When he was almost out of sight, Uzziah spoke.

"Think we'll see that old red nigger again?"

"Acourse," Immanuel said. "Heavens, he'll just show up like he always does," Immanuel said, then added, "Come on, let's get a whiskey and dance with every gal here."

"Sounds like fun."

They walked back in, and no one noticed that Abooksigun had left, but that's the way the old Injun liked it.

They found some Irish whiskey, imagine that, and by the time the music had stopped playing, they had danced with every gal there, and some of them, twice.

STONEWALL JACKSON'S SCOUTS

1

The first they heard of it was when a paddle wheeler came into Wolf Point. There were those on the paddle wheeler who were going any place but back east, where the war was. Confederate troops, under P.G.T. Beauregard, had fired on Fort Sumner the morning of April 11th. Major Robert Anderson, of the Union troops, had been put in charge of the fort when tensions got high. Of course, then, they were just successionists, and nothing more—rebels who could be discounted by simply not counting them, as simple as that.

States had succeeded just after Lincoln's election as President of these United States, and as winter grew into spring, it did not look well for the Union staying together. In fact, most, if not all, of South Carolina knew that it was just a matter of time before the federal properties in the harbor were taken by the rebels. And they were.

Uzziah Ferguson O'Bannon and Immanuel James Jones left on the next paddle wheeler, the one they'd found out about the election, the new war, and all that. When it came back downriver, that's when they left for Virginia. There are few things that tug at a man's heartstrings like the place he was born, few. Immanuel could have cared less, but they were partners, and as such, they were going back to ole Virginny to see what was on the rise.

Father De Smet had left right after Amsterdam Vallon, and both mountain men wondered what would happen there. Jack Tate had settled in with his wife and the majority of Irish who came to stay at Wolf Point. It looked like Buck Krieter, whose wife had had two babies, now ran the majority of the spread for Tate and was becoming, by all means and purposes, a rich man.

Buck had started to swell up with emotion when the boys gave him their cabin, but with two popped out and another on the way, what choice did the boys have?

Booking passage back to St. Louis wasn't hard, most were headed away from the conflict, not toward it.

As they stood on the deck and waved to those who had come down to see them off, mostly the Irish who were glad to be doing something besides stealing, Buck broke down, and his wife had to take him off. She was going to teach that man how to behave if it was the last thing she did.

"Lookie there, pard," Uzziah said, motioning toward where she was leading Buck off the pier, "Buck's ear's gonna hurt for a week."

"Ya know, this is one place I will be glad to be shed of, even ifn it is a war we're goin' to," Immanuel said.

Uzziah was a bit surprised at that statement, he'd always imagined Immanuel happy at Wolf Point, just goes to show you!

"You fellas plan on takin' a room?" It was the captain of the paddle wheeler.

"Yer kinda like an Injun, ain't ya?" Immanuel said as he turned around and saw the short man.

"Yeah, maybe wily, secretive, resourceful, yeah, maybe?" said the man, thinking a compliment had been delivered him.

"That weren't exactly what I meant," Immanuel said.

Not wanting his partner to get involved right away in an argument with one of the uniformed staff, Uzziah changed the subject.

"Yes, yes, we're goin' back to the Ole Dominion," he said using the old-timey vernacular for what some called Virginia.

"Half price on the rooms, just take half off the askin' price and it's yourn," he said and turned and walked away.

"Ya knew I wasn't complimentin' the man, right?"

"Yeah, I know, let's go see what they gots available," Uzziah said, and after having their horses and their pack mules put up, they wandered upstairs.

It turned out to be a very good deal for the two mountain man partners. They got a nice room with a door that led to the balconies, and it was just down from the saloon. After putting their stuff away, they went down to have a drink. The beer was good and cold, and as they sat there drinking and looking out on the balcony, the captain walked by.

"So," he said, not seating himself in deference to their earlier encounter, "how are ya findin' the room?"

Uzziah wasn't usually surprised, but this time, he was.

"Please," Immanuel began, as he pushed with his boot one of the four chairs at the table out for the man, "sit and have a short beer with us."

When Immanuel looked at Uzziah, his mouth was open.

"Is it fly season?" Immanuel asked Uzziah, who promptly shut his mouth.

The captain flicked his wrist and the man at the bar brought him his usual, which turned out to be mineral water.

"A man who pilots this much weight can't be too careful," he said as he raised his glass of seltzer to them, and they, their beers.

"We need to know what's going on in St. Louis, sir," Immanuel said.

"First introductions, I'm Captain Peter Strauss, and you are?"

"That's my partner, Uzziah Ferguson O'Bannon, and I'm Immanuel James Jones."

"Why are ya goin' east?" the captain asked.

"Why not?" Jones asked.

"That won't do if the authorities question you in St. Louis."

"What do you mean?" Uzziah asked.

"The situation there is tenuous to say the least. With the recent influx of mostly German and Irish immigrants, and the Union trying to pick up on them, there's not a lot of room left over for southern sympathizers."

Immanuel and Uzziah exchanged a quick look, and the die, so to speak, was cast.

"We're returning to my father's home in Baltimore," Immanuel said.

"Thought he said ya was going to Ole Dominion?"

"Well, we're gonna pass through there on our way to Maryland," Immanuel offered.

"Well, that's a bit like saying you're returning to Missouri. I mean, Maryland is close to the capital, but just across the Potomac, there's secessionist Virginia," Captain Strauss said as he sipped his mineral water.

"Uzziah, where are you from?" The captain was getting way too personal with all these questions.

"He was born out west on the Upper Missouri," Immanuel said.

"Where on the Upper?"

"Fort Mandan." Uzziah had been ready with that response, and it seemed to please the German captain very much.

"Well, I have duties and cannot, although it's been lovely, spend as much time chatting with passengers as I'd like," he said, finishing thc mineral water. "Good day, gentlemen," he said, setting the empty glass down and leaving the salon.

"Damn! Did that man ask a lot of questions, or what?" Immanuel asked, looking after the captain.

"Yeah, well, I think things are goin' to get way different afore this is all through," Uzziah said, looking at his partner.

"Ya really think so?"

"Yeah, old son, this country is at war with itself. There will be long-forgotten injustices that will be remembered. Neighbor will turn on neighbor, and—I don't know, I think it's gonna get real ugly."

"Why? 'Cause some want to have slaves and others don't?"

"That's part of it, but when given an excuse, well, people will do the damndest things."

They spent the rest of the voyage sort of secluded. If they came out at all, it was when the early morning hours as the revelers, and there seemed to be a sense of false revelry to most of it, those people were rarely seen in the early morning hours, and those were the hours the boys liked the most.

To just sit back against the boiler room wall, listen to the engines, and watch the river pass by. They didn't have much to say, till one day Immanuel spoke up.

"Hey, lookie, ain't that where we jumped the ship at the wood station, then sat up there on the small hill and shot the shite out of that paddle wheel?"

Uzziah stood and looked out to that prominence, and yes, it was the exact spot where Immanuel and he had disabled the paddle wheeler and left Kate Warne and her Pinkerton Agent man spinning in the current.

"Yep, yep, that's the spot. Sometimes ya don't realize how far a shot ya made was till ya see it from the other end," Uzziah said.

They stayed out of the saloons after that, even though Immanuel wanted to gamble, but his old penchant for wanting to drink seemed to have been stemmed by the time they had spent at Wolf Point. Regardless, they kept to themselves, and whenever they saw the captain, it seemed to both of them that the man was looking askance at them. Maybe they were being restless and uneasy for no reason. All they knew was that when they got to the docks at St. Louis, they couldn't have been happier to be leading Stygian and Shadow off the ship and onto the docks. They had sat up half the night with anticipation, and when it docked earlier than most thought it would, they were there at the stable and tipping the stable boy big to let them into the stalls and saddle their own horses and get their gear properly placed on the horses.

They rode to the Growling Catfish, and sure enough, there was Uzziah's old boss standing out in front of the place smoking his pipe.

"Charlie Watts!" Uzziah yelled as he jumped down from Shadow and picked the older man up and spun him in a circle.

"Hey! Hey!" Charlie protested until Uzziah sat him down.

"Uzziah?"

"Ain't nobody quite as ugly," Uzziah said of himself.

"Well, that's true," Watts said as he puffed on his pipe and looked from under his brow at the man he'd hired when Uzziah had first come to St. Louis, then Watts's attention shifted to the other dark horse, "Immanuel James Jones!?!"

"That what they call me!" Immanuel said proudly, but Watts whispered behind his hand to Uzziah, "What happened to him?"

"Come on down, Charlie says he'll treat us to breakfast, and pussy!" Uzziah yelled over to Immanuel.

"I never said nothin' 'bout the other thing," Charlie said, and the two mountain men chuckled as they followed Charlie into the Growling Catfish.

It looked much as it had so many years before. Sleepy soiled doves were coming from the back and getting their chicory coffee, yawning, and talking with each other about the goings on of the night before. They were staring at the two big mountain men.

"Ladies, it ain't polite to stare!" Charlie said, and they went back to their conversations.

"I don't see no one from before," Uzziah said.

"No, they come here, they either die or they graduate to somethin' else," Watts said, then snapped his fingers at one of the girls and she brought over coffee.

"Thank you," Immanuel said.

"Ya bet, grandpa," she said as she set the other cup in front of Uzziah, who could barely contain himself.

"Grandpa's money's as good as anyone's, little girl," Immanuel said in his own defense.

"Ya want a poke after breakfast, old man, just say so," she said as she sashayed away.

"Tell Cookie, two big breakfasts, the works," Charlie yelled after her. She didn't turn, but just stuck an index finger into the air and kept on walking.

Uzziah was sipping his cup and sneaking a look at Immanuel.

"What ya lookin' at?!?"

"Nothin', gramps," Uzziah said, chuckling to himself.

"Are the soiled doves gettin' younger?" Immanuel asked Charlie.

That was it, Uzziah spat the mouthful of coffee halfway across the table.

"That's it! Stand up and prepare yerself for a beatin'," Immanuel said, jumping up and taking the position of a pugilist.

"I ain't gonna fight ya, grandpa," Uzziah said, setting his coffee back down. The whole time, the whores and Charlie were enjoying the show.

"Don't call me that!" Immanuel insisted.

"Oh, sorry, I apologize...it's great-grandpa, ain't it!?"

That was it, Immanuel leaped from where he was standing and landed on his partner. They rolled around on the floor, and one of the soiled doves actually said, "I got $5 on the old man!"

Immanuel looked up to see which one it was when Uzziah landed a right across his chin, and he went down and out.

"Oops," Uzziah said as he got up off the floor and placed Immanuel's jacket under his head.

The whore who had bet on Immanuel handed the five bucks to the other soiled dove.

"Is he okay?" Watts asked, seemingly concerned.

"When he wakes, he'll be mad as a hare, but he's breathin' good," Uzziah said, putting his hand on Immanuel's chest. "Yeah, he's fine."

"He looks different," Charlie said.

Uzziah sat back down but kept his eyes on his partner.

"Yeah, well, as it says in Ecclesiastes, '*Time and chance happeneth to them all*,'" Uzziah quoted.

"All these years and ya still stickin' with the Good Book," Charlie said, smiling.

"Ya know what BIBLE means, don't ya?" Uzziah asked.

"Best Information Before Leaving Earth," Immanuel said from the floor.

"He's awake," Charlie said, like he was glad grandpa hadn't been seriously hurt.

Immanuel sat up and rubbed his jaw. "Damn, son, what ya hittin' me that hard fer?"

"If ya hadn't been worried 'bout the soiled dove who bet on ya, ya wouldn't have looked away," Uzziah said, then added, "Hey, come on, partner, here's breakfast." Reaching down without getting out of his chair, he pulled Immanuel up to his chair.

2

At the beginning of the Civil War, President Lincoln called upon Missouri to supply the Union with four regiments. Governor Jackson of Missouri, a strong southern sympathizer, refused the President and ordered the Missouri state militia to muster outside St. Louis so they could train for home defense.

In March of that same year, Captain Nathaniel Lyon arrived in St. Louis and took command of Company B of the 2nd Infantry Regiment. Fearing that Governor Jackson had taken arms and supplies for his home guard, the captain disguised himself as a farm woman and went out to see what the militia was up to. As it turned out, he spotted several cannons that belonged to the US government, obviously stolen from the arsenal.

Captain Lyon, fearing that the governor of Missouri was going to use those cannons against the Union, armed from that same arsenal a paramilitary group that was pro-Union. They were called the Wide Awakes.

The captain then moved the rest of the arsenal across the river to Illinois. He quickly led the Wide Awakes to the governor's camp and forced them to surrender. Captain Lyon decided it would be a good idea to march those prisoners in daylight through the streets of St. Louis to help stanch any other opposition to the Union.

Immanuel and Uzziah were making their way to the train station in order to buy tickets and travel to Virginia. They had no idea that, as they made their way early that morning in the direction of the depot, using the same road they had used many times before that a group of prisoners was about to intersect their path.

"Well," Immanuel said as they lazily trotted their horses along, "Guess St. Louie ain't as torn up about this chere comin' war as we suspected."

The sound of a crowd met their ears, and it was coming from the right on the road that intersected the one they were on. Both men perked up in the saddle and decided it would probably be best to be on the other side of what was coming before it happened.

They clicked up their mounts, and as they made the cross street, they could see a rather big crowd, possibly even a mob, as they followed what looked like military troops. The troops were encircling a lot of men, who were bound and headed someplace where authorities deal with such things.

As they made the cross street, both partners pulled up and tucked their horses behind a hay wagon that was sitting on the side of the street and looked in safety as the entourage walked past.

"What the hell?!?" Immanuel yelled so that Uzziah could hear him. "What ya suppose that's all 'bout!?"

Uzziah was about to answer when the crowd started throwing rocks and bottles at the military types. Right there in the intersection they had just crossed, the crowd gathered in the street and continued to pummel the troops.

The first shot came from somewhere other than the troops, but the front line, dropping down on one knee, and the second line of troops behind, both opened up on the crowd.

What they saw next reminded them that the city that had wanted their scalps for killing an undersheriff hadn't changed that much in the years since. Women, children, young boys, and men were hurled to the ground as lead traveled through their bodies. At one point, they thought, surely, it's over now, but the troops reloaded and fired again at the backs of the fleeing civilians, more casualties went down.

"We gotta do somethin'!" Immanuel protested.

"Yeah, get the hell outta here!" Uzziah said and kicked Shadow away from the melee.

In the background, the firing continued as the two mountain men made their way toward the train yards.

"The depot's that way," Immanuel reminded his partner.

"Yeah, do yaw wanna get a ticket when things like that are happenin'?"

"Well, hell, we can't ride all the way," Immanuel said.

"Who says?" Uzziah said as he pulled Shadow up alongside a boxcar and pulled the doors open.

Minutes later, they had found boarding planks and

led the horses and themselves to safety. No sooner had they done so than the freight train they had boarded jerked and then was underway. They loosely tied their horses to the planks along the side of the boxcar, then sat down in the hay. Well, they didn't have to worry about feeding those horses, that's for sure.

As the train gained speed going east out of St. Louis, they sat back on the stacks of hay and looked at each other.

"Brother, that was murder back there," Immanuel commented.

"Ya think?"

"Bottles and rocks against bullets, yeah, I'd say so!"

"Now what do ya think 'bout this war?" Uzziah asked.

"Ya got me," Immanuel said, giving up.

"What just happened back there will be forgotten in the battles that are to come. Bodies stacked like cordwood, limbs chopped off by doctors from both sides as they practice their medicine and try to save lives."

"Maybe we shoulda stayed in Wolf Point?" Immanuel said, pulling out his smoking materials, then realizing there was so much hay around, he put them back.

"Maybe?" Uzziah said, wishing he could smoke, too, but knowing the dangers.

They traveled into the night, and even the horses laid down for a bit as they tried to get as comfortable as possible. The boys never traveled without two canteens, just in case, and this was a perfect case in point.

In the middle of the night, Immanuel dreamed that he was back at the Pere Gros sweat lodge, stumbling around and trying to make sense of what he saw. The pain, he remembered the pains in his chest, and the way the center pole was pulling on him as he put one foot in front of the other, then he had a flash of something else, something which he had forgotten until that very dream.

It was toward the end, when the hooks had torn his flesh and he had almost fallen but was caught by someone. He was thinking in the dream that it was Uzziah who had caught him? As he went out into the day and those who had participated in the dance were down at the river washing all the paint off their bodies. He went down as he had that day, and when he turned, the man—the Injun, who had hugged him so tenderly—turned, and there was a tomahawk in his hand, and this time there wasn't going to be any hugs!

When he awakened, it was plain to see that what was coming was going to resemble the dream. Those who had previously been amicable to one another were no longer going to be that way. There were articles in a paper he'd read that said that the war would be over in the first big battle, but he thought that that was rather presumptuous of the writer and felt that when he'd read the article that it had been written to soothe the situation instead of dealing with it as it was coming on. He wondered how that same writer might feel now that men, women, and children—all unarmed—had been shot down on the streets of St. Louis?

In the morning, they had no idea how far they'd come, but they must be getting close to a depot because the train was slowing down. Uzziah took the liberty of opening the door slightly and getting some fresh air into the boxcar. The horses snorted appreciatively, and Immanuel came and stood behind his partner.

Up ahead was an incline that was leading into the mountains. It could only be the Appalachian Range, and perhaps when they made it over those mountains, they would be in the Shenandoah Valley?

"Could we have traveled this far?" Immanuel asked from behind Uzziah.

"I don't know, maybe. Anyways, there will probably be a water stop somewhere up this way."

"Ya think it's best to get off?" Immanuel asked.

"Depends."

"On what?"

"On whether they check the cars when they stop for water."

They'd made one grade, and before they started up the next, there was this flat area, a little town, and it looked a whole lot like this was their water stop.

As they watched, from their boxcar, they could see that the train bulls, the brakemen who liked to throw bums from the trains, were starting up high by the engine and working their way back toward them.

"I'm guessin' this is where we get off?" Immanuel said as he walked back to Stygian and tightened the latigo and readjusted the saddle. He did the same for Uzziah.

"Ya think we mighta left something?" Uzziah asked.

"Nah, frankly. I'm glad. Never wanted a smoke so bad."

The place where their boxcar had stopped offered flat ground and grassy slopes down off the railroad easement.

"Ya ready?" Uzziah asked.

Immanuel nodded, and Uzziah pulled the door all the way back. It was barely in place when Immanuel and Stygian shot from the doorway to the grassy knoll just off the easement. Uzziah could already hear shouts from the brakeman and a pistol shot. Damn! Things were getting serious around this war!

He jumped Shadow—who would do about anything Uzziah wanted, within reason—off the boxcar, and an angry bee buzzed by his head in the middle of the jump. That was close!

Instinctively, he whipped out his revolver and did a snapshot back at the bull, who threw both his arms in the air and rolled down the embankment.

As they galloped away, Immanuel turned to Uzziah.

"Damn young son, that was some fine shottin'!" he yelled over to Uzziah, as both men hunched over their saddles in case someone else got trigger happy.

"Didn't mean to hit 'im," Uzziah tried to explain.

"Well, I'm sure he didn't mean to die!"

The town turned out to be Parkersburg, which lay along the confluence of the Ohio and the Little Kanawha Rivers. They skirted the town, and that was a good thing since Parkersburg was quickly becoming a staging for the Union army, and eventually MacMillan himself would stage strikes against the Confederacy from that point.

As it was, it took the two mountain men partners five days to finally reach the Shenandoah Valley. They decided that once they got to Beverly, Virginia, which was about halfway, they needed a hot meal, a warm bed, and some supplies.

As they rode down the main street of Beverly, they noticed a brick mercantile building, which was unusual for a small town. It was the Blackman-Bosworth Store and was the first such building west of the Allegheny Mountains.

There was plenty of buying and selling going on, and Immanuel and Uzziah, dressed as they were in their deerskins, seemed to attract a lot of attention. It got so that at one point that Immanuel started waving to those who gawked and saying hello. Most of this was met with people quickly looking away, and no one speaking to him.

"Guessin' they just wanna gawk!" Immanuel said loudly.

"Why don't you pull it back a notch. We need supplies, and such, and we probably shouldn't be making spectacles of ourselves," Uzziah warned, not wanting really to attract too much attention.

"In the Rockies or on the Missouri, we're just people, but here looks like we might be special folk," Immanuel said, smiling at those who still gawked.

They spotted the hostlers and rode down to it, dismounting out front. A man who must be the owner, or certainly someone who worked there, simply came out and looked at the two horses.

"Wanna sell 'em?" he asked in a strong Virginia accent.

"Does it look like we wanna sell 'em?" Immanuel came back gruffly.

"I can sell these chere hosses fer ya, fer sure!"

"We want ya to feed 'em, check their shoes, and find 'em a stall," Uzziah said politely.

"So, yer the civil one, huh?" the man said, looking all the while at Immanuel, who stared back at him as if he wanted to kill him.

"Good café around?" Uzziah asked, trying to get the two idiots out of the staring contest.

"Yeah, yeah," he said, still staring at Immanuel, then he looked over at Uzziah. "Just down the street, about two blocks, ifn ya miss it, yer blind. Payment for stalls and feeding upfront, then we'll talk 'bout their shoes," he ended up saying.

Uzziah flipped him a coin, which he adroitly caught and pocketed without even looking at it.

"Is that 'nuff?" Uzziah asked.

"I'm sure it is," the man said as he took the reins from them and walked them back into the stables.

They walked the boardwalk until they saw the café on the same side of the street. Uzziah held the door for Immanuel.

Inside, the place was about three-quarters filled. They took a seat in the back with their backs to the wall on both sides. The waitress, who was young and good-looking, brought the menus. Immanuel started thinking differently about Beverly, Virginia.

"My, my, y'all look authentic!" she said as she handed them the menus.

"Well, we is, darlin', we is!" Immanuel said, giving the young lady a smile that Uzziah had not seen in a long time.

"Something to drink afore ya order?" she asked.

"Ya got—"

"Coffee, we'll both have coffee," Uzziah said, interrupting Immanuel, who turned and looked at Uzziah.

"Sure," she said and turned her perky little arse around, and went for the coffee. Immanuel continued to stare at Uzziah.

"Yer missin' a nice exit," Uzziah reminded him.

"Since when do ya order fer me?"

"Every time I cook fer ya," Uzziah said, noticing several tables turning and staring at them. He guessed they were *authentic*, as the waitress had said, and that maybe this particular look had died years ago in this part of Virginia—at least in town.

Immanuel started to say something, but the waitress returned with some really big mugs of steaming coffee and set them down in front of both men.

"Thank ya, darlin'," Immanuel said, flashing that smile again.

"Sure," she said and turned and walked away. This time, Immanuel did not miss the exit.

When Immanuel stopped watching, it was only when the waitress went to another table with an order. By that time, he'd drunk half the hot coffee and was smiling.

"Good and hot coffee, ain't it, partner?" Uzziah asked.

"Not as hot as those puppies fighting under the backend of her dress," Immanuel said.

Uzziah just smiled. He was glad that Immanuel was getting back to being his old self again, as long as that didn't include getting drunk.

The menu was extensive, well, when it came to getting something different—when Uzziah cooked, he fixed whatever he fixed, and now there was a veritable smorgasbord in front of them—well, at least on paper.

"Where are we, New York?" Immanuel said as he read the menu.

"Lots a choices, huh, partner?"

"What ya gonna have, we shouldn't git the same things so we can try more than one item, huh?"

Uzziah simply shook his head.

"What's ya shaking yer head fer?"

"Nothin'."

"Nah, it meant somethin' what?"

The waitress came back. "Do ya know what ya want?" Unfortunately, an open-ended question that Uzziah thought he'd better get in front of before they really got into trouble.

"I'll have the meatloaf," Uzziah said.

"That comes with mash and beans, okay?"

"Sure, fine," Uzziah said, setting the menu down on the table.

"How 'bout ya?" she said, turning toward Immanuel.

"How 'bout me?" Immanuel said, smiling that ridiculous smile again.

She looked at him, confused at first, then realized this old man was possibly flirting with her. She blushed and looked down at the table away from Immanuel's searching gaze.

Uzziah kicked Immanuel under the table.

"That's my leg!" Immanuel protested.

"I know!" was all Uzziah said.

"What would ya eat ifn ya was orderin'?" Immanuel asked the girl.

"I like the steak," she said eagerly.

"Well, that's what I'll have," he said.

"How ya want that cooked?"

"Just knock the horns off."

"Ya got good choppers?" she asked.

"What?!?"

"It's easier to eat ifn it's cooked a bit," she said, smiling mildly.

"These are mine," Immanuel said as he tapped on his front teeth with the fingernail on his index finger, "if that's what yer worried 'bout?"

"Rare it is, then," she said, and how 'bout the taters and beans?"

"Yeah, that's fine," he said, calming down a bit.

The waitress left and Uzziah was chuckling to himself.

"Don't!" Immanuel said.

"Don't what?"

"Don't laugh at me!"

"Partner, yer just one funny man to be with."

"Is that supposed to be a compliment?"

"No, just a fact," Uzziah said, picking up his silverware and shining it with his cloth napkin.

They managed to stop arguing, which was a thing in itself. If they had been out on the plains or back home, what was being said might just turn into fisticuffs, with them rolling around in the campfire. You just never knew with those two. But they were almost home, the Shenandoah was just over the Allegany Mountains, then it was a simple ride down the valley to his pa's place. So, both men sat there having their coffee cups filled with excellent coffee, and maybe that was what made the difference. By the time their meals arrived, Immanuel was settled down enough to eat, and he ate well. The steak must have been tender, or he ate it just to prove he had good choppers! You could never tell with that man.

While they were eating, Uzziah's mind went to the war that was already on, and his six brothers. He knew how faithful they were to Virginia, and he imagined they'd all be joining the new Confederacy and fighting. He couldn't help but wonder how many would be killed. His daddy was probably too old to fight, and that was good. He hated the thought of Rahab becoming a widow at her age. The only one he had second thoughts about was Obadiah. He could see the young man running to his caves, hiding out until the conflict was ended. But who knew, really? There was a strong family feeling about the Shenandoah Valley, and the valley existed in the heart of Virginia.

They paid their bill. Uzziah gaped at the tip that his partner had left the waitress, whose name they now knew to be Gertrude, a German name. Uzziah knew plenty of Germans who had come over and settled in the Shenandoah Valley.

"Where to now, partner?" Immanuel asked.

"Let's get rooms, ifn we got enough money after that there tip," Uzziah said, and when they found the two hotels in town which Gertrude had told them about, they decided to stay at the first one. They were across the street from one another, but the first offered breakfast as part of the deal—a coupon which could be used at Gertrude's café.

The rooms were nice and adjoining through a door on the connecting wall. They had a balcony with rocking chairs on it, and after they'd sat down what their saddlebags had in them, they wandered out there and had a seat. It was private enough—all the rooms along the front had doors which emptied onto it, but that was just five rooms, which meant ten rockers. There was no one out there that early, so they packed their pipes, pulled their slouch hats down to block the sun, and smoked.

"There's a saloon across the way," Immanuel said. He was a bloodhound when it came to places that served whiskey.

"Sure is," Uzziah said lazily. The breakfast had taken his edge off, and sitting there in the morning sun was making him sleepy.

When he awakened, his pipe had fallen to the floor of the balcony, and Immanuel was nowhere to be seen. He was getting his head back on straight when he heard shouting from across the street at the Watering Hole, the saloon Immanuel had noticed. One of the voices he recognized, and he was fairly sure it was Immanuel.

Locking both rooms, he hurried down the stairs to the lobby, where several men were standing at the window looking across the street.

By the time he made the boardwalk in front of the hotel, a figure came flying out of the saloon between the batwing doors. It was not Immanuel, but he followed shortly afterward, and was putting a tongue-lashing on the younger man who now lay in the street.

"The next time ya decide to call a man something that he don't like, maybe ya'll think twice about it!" Immanuel said, standing over the young fella.

"I didn't mean nothin' by it," the man protested, and started to get up.

"Like hell!" Immanuel said and kicked the young man in the head, sending him back to reclining on the street.

Quite a crowd had gathered, and Uzziah wondered how he was going to get Immanuel out of this trouble when a man with a pistol came out of the batwings and aimed the thing at Immanuel.

A loud boom brought everyone to turning in the direction of its origin after, of course, they had watched the man with the gun fly through the Watering Hole's front plate glass window. There stood Uzziah with smoke roiling from the barrel of his Hawken.

"Put it down!" a voice yelled from the opposite boardwalk. There was a man with a star on his vest, standing there with a pistol, drawn, cocked, and loaded, pointed at Uzziah.

3

What were they to do? These were the times when it paid to have been partners as long as they had been. Sure, Uzziah could surrender, or at least appear to surrender, and then could be taken to jail. They had been through similar situations with one or the other of them eventually behind bars. It wasn't like they were crooks. They weren't. They were honest, hard-working men who just got into situations that called for a little ingenuity. Well, that was the way they looked at it.

What they both remembered at this point was that this was not the Wild West. The sheriff, or marshal, or whomever he was, was a man who had most likely been elected—a politician. And the good people who elected him were standing around him, but were they behind him?

Both mountain men looked at each other, and without words being spoken, they made their move. Obviously, the Hawken was empty and would have to be reloaded, so Immanuel put his back against the saloon's outside wall and pulled his revolver.

"Throw it down, Sheriff," Immanuel said.

The man looked at him and couldn't quite believe his ears.

"What'd ya say, old man?" the sheriff said as he began to turn the pistol in Immanuel's direction.

"I will drop ya where ya stand!" Immanuel whispered just loud enough for the sheriff and Uzziah to hear.

To a greater extent than not, it must have convinced the sheriff, for he did drop his gun. Being practical men, Immanuel rushed over, picked up the sheriff's pistol, and taking him hostage, went out to Uzziah.

"Ya grab our stuff from the room, and I'll hold this one in case any of the good citizens of Beverly get a notion," Immanuel whispered to Uzziah.

Uzziah ran into the hotel and did just that. By the time he got back outside, there was quite a crowd, and they weren't being civil. Well, half of them were drunk, and that didn't help, including Immanuel, whose breath was just about enough to intoxicate Uzziah.

The hostler's was down to the right, so they took the sheriff down an alley between two buildings, and they could hear men shouting behind them.

"Come on! Let's get them!" someone yelled, but so far it was just shouts. When a kicked-in-the-head, knocked-out friend or foe lies dead just outside the batwing doors, it discouraged bravery to a greater extent than anything two men dressed in deerskins could have.

They got to the back of the hostlers—it was open to the back—and went in. The hostler stepped out with a lantern and held it up to see what was going on.

"Sheriff," the hostler said.

"Dan," the sheriff said in an even voice.

"What's goin' on?" he asked the sheriff. He had yet to see the gun in the sheriff's back.

"Saddle up Wakefield and the horses that belong to these gentlemen, please," the sheriff requested in an even voice.

"I re-shoed one horse and they ain't paid—"

A coin spun through the air, and even in the lamplight, the hostler was able to fetch it from the darkness.

"Yes, sir!" the hostler said.

So far, the crowd that had supposedly followed them was nowhere to be seen.

"I'm riden' with you Yankee scum out of town, just don't shoot nobody else," the sheriff whispered out of the side of his mouth.

"Who ya callin' Yankees!?!" Uzziah asked none too politely.

The hostler came out with all three horses saddled.

"That was fast," the sheriff commented.

"Just loosened the latigoes on the strangers' horses," was the explanation.

They rode out the back of the hostlers and down the alley toward the south. They didn't gallop, just a nice dogtrot, until they got to the end of town.

"This is as far as I'm goin'," the sheriff said.

"That's fine by us, but why ya being so nice?" Uzziah asked.

"Now, I'm confused, that's a Virginie accent ifn I ever heard one," the sheriff admitted.

"I'm from Ole Dominion, I am. Again, why ya helpin' us?"

"The man ya kilt was a no-good son of a bitch and a

woman beater. Nobody gonna be unhappy about his death, certainly not his wife and three abused kids."

The boys just looked at each other and shrugged. The sheriff's pistol was emptied on the road, and thrown down, then they were off. They had forgotten about his Winchester, which he drew from the saddle holster and aimed down their retreating trail, but the twilight had swallowed them.

They rode for the next hour, putting as much room between them and Beverly as they could. Finally, they crossed into the Shenandoah Valley. They rode till they saw a stream, and while the horses were watering, Uzziah finally spoke.

"Looks like good water, ya want yer canteen filled?" he said as he got down off Shadow and just dropped the reins on the bank.

"Yeah. Thanks," was all Immanuel said, then he handed the canteen to Uzziah, and as he tried to take it, held it there between them. "Sorry 'bout that."

"Yeah, me too," Uzziah said, and Immanuel let him take the canteen. "Say who was the guy who was 'bout to back shoot ya?"

"Have no idea."

"Really, seems a wild thing to do to somebody ya don't know."

"Yeah, no kiddin'," Immanuel said, pulling his pipe out and filling the bowl.

Uzziah knelt by the stream and made sure he kept the neck of the canteen upstream and out of any muddy water.

"So, the man in the street—the younger man, I might add—the one ya whipped up on, who was he?"

"Just somebody who didn't like the way I looked, I guess."

"What'd he say to ya?" Uzziah asked as he handed the filled canteen from his saddle horn and held out Immanuel's to him.

"Something 'bout my Yankee accent, then threw in a few choice words about my parentage."

"He was drunk?"

"He was."

"And you?"

"Had me two whiskeys and didn't even get to finish the second one," Immanuel said, looking away.

"Two?"

"Maybe three, I don't 'member. Say, thanks for saving my bacon back there."

"And you mine, the last time one of us ended up in jail, except when the Pinkertons were tellin' all their lies, somebody almost got hung."

"Buried is what I got!"

"Still a sore subject, is it?"

"Yeah, partner, still."

"I dug ya up."

Travelers came along the same road they were on, and Uzziah raised a friendly hand.

"Howdy," the man said. He was with a young woman, maybe his daughter, maybe his wife.

Both partners watched as they rode up the way they had just come down, then Uzziah mounted up.

"Let's get the hell home," Uzziah said as he mounted up and they took off in a dogtrot down the road.

They spent the next few days traveling as fast as they could without raising suspicions of anyone else along the way. They stayed to the forests and mountains, and finally, when the O'Bannon farm came into view, they were to the west and in the hills, about the same place where the Army sniper used by the Pinkertons had taken a shot at them those years before.

"Well, there she is," Immanuel said.

"Yeah, but let me see the glass, will ya?" Uzziah asked, and Immanuel got the binoculars from his saddlebags and handed them to Uzziah.

He had the glasses at his eyes for some time before he lowered them.

"Everything okay?" Immanuel asked.

"No, no, it's not. The place looks like it's goin' to seed, there's equipment scattered everywhere."

"Well, let's go see what's goin' on," Immanuel said.

They rode down out of the hills, cautious and their heads on swivels. When they made the main road, they rode the short distance down it until they turned down the long drive that led to the O'Bannon farmhouse. Uzziah's heart was palpitating, and his stomach had butterflies in it.

"What's scaring ya?" Immanuel asked.

"It just ain't right. The whole place looks scattered about," Uzziah said as he saw Rahab, his ma, coming out of the side door to the house with a basket full of wet laundry.

"Well, yer ma's okay," Immanuel remarked.

The scene that happened then has happened a million times over in history. Young men and women return home to find the love that's always there, but now things were akimbo, things were just off kilter.

Uzziah rode up hard in front of Immanuel, jumping off his horse while Shadow was still walking, and letting the reins go, he ran into Rahab's arms. She held him tight, and Immanuel could see in her face the strain that she was under.

"Darlin' Uzziah, darlin' Uzziah," Rahab said as she refused to let go of her oldest son.

"Where's Pa?" Uzziah finally asked as he broke from the hug.

"Come inside, will ya," Rahab said, not letting go of Uzziah's hand.

"Don't worry, I'll put the hosses up," Immanuel said.

Rahab walked Uzziah over to Immanuel, where he stood with both sets of reins in his hand. Letting go of Uzziah, she held Immanuel and whispered in his ear, "You look different, but still good," she said as they hugged.

Immanuel kissed her on the cheek. "I'll be in as soon as the horses are put up," he said. "Great to see ya, Rahab, you look even younger than ya did the last time I saw ya," Immanuel said, meaning every word of it.

"Ya flattering fool, on ya go now," she said as she slapped at his arm.

As Immanuel walked to the barn, he could hear the squeals and screams of Uzziah's sisters. He tried to remember exactly who they were. *Women especially loved to be remembered,* he thought. *Let's see,* he thought as he took the horses into the large stalls, unsaddled them, and looked for the hay. There was Sally, he wasn't sure he'd meet her the last time, she'd gotten married and moved off, then there was Hanna, red-headed and fiery, his favorite of all the O'Bannon sisters, of course, there was Sarah, who was wonderful, and Faith, only fifteen years old the last time he'd seen her.

Now all these sisters would be what? At least five years older, and really into womanhood. Well, he wouldn't cross any boundaries that he weren't asked to cross. He chided himself for thinking like that, but he was Immanuel James Jones, and women held a place in his heart, a place like no other. When he dreamed, he dreamed of them, when he went about, he noticed them, when in his remanences he thought of them all reverently.

There was a squeal and a rushing from the barn door, and Faith, who was only fifteen the last time he saw her, came running toward him with all the grace and beauty of a blue-eyed day, all smiles, and arms extended. He picked her up and swung her in a circle.

"Is it really you, Immanuel?" she asked, then added, "So much slimmer and muscular."

God, he loved to be complimented by good-looking female stock.

"It's me, but I'm sorry I don't recognize ya," he said as he broke from their hug, but kept his arms around her.

"You know who I am, you will always know who I am," she said, and she was right. Her beauty had blossomed into womanhood, and his heart skipped a beat just to look at her. God, she was beautiful, ole Sean O'Bannon and his wife Rahab made beautiful babies!

"Of course, Faith, you are without a doubt a beauty," Immanuel said, and as a reward, she kissed him on the cheek, let go of him, took his hand, and started leading him from the barn.

"Where's the hay?" he asked her.

She ran over to where the hay was, threw it haphazardly into the stalls, rejoined him and, taking his hand, led him from the barn, talking all the while.

Standing in the barn with the hay on them, covering their backs and flanks, Shadow and Stygian stood there as complacent as could be, eating what had fallen down in front of them. They could hear the female's chatter as the two humans left the barn.

"This war will be the death of us, Immanuel, it will," she said in her honeycombed Virginia accent.

4

Immanuel guessed correctly that once they entered the house, he would no longer be hers. The others, Uzziah's sisters, all ran to meet him when he entered the back way through the kitchen. Sally was nearly in her thirties, but still with the hair of gold, and the smile that carried you for days, then came Hanna, the red-headed cyclone, then a girl he hadn't remembered, must be Sarah, who was off at art school the last time they were there, and finally, he had Faith already on his dominant arm.

They made over him, shoving cups of lemonade and cookies into his hands, as he sat down in the parlor, where a warming fire was welcomed, and it was joyous, but Immanuel knew melancholy when he encountered it, and these women were starving for male company, and he was soon to find out why.

"Ma has been telling me everything, and the others are fillin' in," Uzziah said.

"What's the upshot?" Immanuel asked.

"Well, Pa and the boys decided that they had better fight for their homeland of Virginia. Obadiah wanted to go a course, but after Ma and Pa had a talk, it was decided that he couldn't go, not being in the state of mind that he was usually in, so, after Pa and the boys left, he stayed a couple days, then ran off. They thought he'd gone to his caves, but when Sally rode out there, nothing."

"The fires hadn't been lit, and there was no sign of Obadiah havin' been there," Sally said.

"We were frantic, a course," Ma Rahab said, "and Sally wanted to go lookin' fer him up north, but that was simply foolish, and I convinced her, along with all her sisters, that that way was nothin' but trouble fer her."

"Well," Immanuel said, taking Sally's hand, "I'm glad ya didn't go. A purty woman like yerself, no tellin' what woulda happened."

"They're off to join the Confederacy, there's talk of the first battle of the war, somewhere west of Washington," Sally chimed in.

During an hour and a half of conversation, they found out—the two mountain men did—that once Fort Sumter happened that passions were riding hot throughout Virginia. And when Colonel Robert Edward Lee had refused the command offered to him by Lincoln of the entire Union army, and he had accepted the command of the Army of the Confederacy, well, there had been a rush to enlist. At first all the O'Bannon boys wanted to join the cavalry, but cooler heads prevailed as their father, Sean, had convinced them that the real war would be in the infantry, and if they joined together, they would probably be allowed to enlist in the same regiment, and protect each other, so they had left for Winchester, Virginia, to see who would be needing them.

"So, there's no word on where they will fight, or who they joined up with?" Uzziah finally asked.

"No," Rahab said. "As you can imagine, communications have been disrupted since the mail service belonged to the Union. It will take time afore other mail services will be available."

"They got themselves, the Confederacy, a Post Office Department as early as February this year," Hanna said, "but the mail's spotty at best."

"Girls, girls, one of ya go out to the barn, and slaughter one of the smaller pigs, it's gonna be pork loin, sweet taters, green beans for these young men!" Rahab said, and the whole room went into action.

"I'll help ya peel the potatoes, Ma," Uzziah said.

"Well, please wash those hands first," she said.

"I see nothin' changed around chere," Uzziah said, following his ma into their kitchen.

Immanuel sat there wondering what was happening at his father's house in Baltimore. Wondering if they had stayed in New Orleans, or come home, and whose side they would be on. He imagined they would all side with the North, since Baltimore was so close to Washington, but who knew?

He had to admit that being with all these women, and realizing that all their brothers, sons, and their father and husband having gone off to the war was a shock to him, and he surely knew that it had sent shock waves throughout the entire family.

Mama Rahab, the name that only Uzziah called his mother, fixed his favorite meal of fresh pork loin, sweet potatoes, and green beans from the garden. The meal was as it always was—fabulous. Uzziah's mouth started to water right before he cut into the loin.

"Don't slobber on the pork, sweetie," Mama Rahab had said, and all the girls, and Immanuel, too, laughed. Uzziah took his sleeve and wiped away the drool that was coming.

"Ya know how much I like this, Mama Rahab, can't help meself," Uzziah said, smiling like he was seven years old again.

That night, as the household that had become so active with their brother and oldest son returning with his partner of over ten years settled into a peaceful sleep, Immanuel and Uzziah sat in front of the fireplace downstairs and had decided that they would best serve the family if they were in the part of the house that would be entered if someone were trespassing.

Their pipes going, they sat in rockers in front of the fire as the four sisters and the mother of Uzziah were sleeping upstairs. They heard something on the stairs and, turning their heads, there stood Sally, her golden tresses falling on each side of her nightgown. She wore slippers, and if it had been anyone else downstairs, she might have been able to sneak up on them.

"You heard me," she said, surprised that they had seen her.

"Well, yeah, a course," Uzziah said.

"I guess that's one of the things that makes you a frontiersman," she continued as she came over and sat on the milking stool that sat near the fire.

Both her brother and his partner nodded in agreement.

"Look, I can't tell you what it means for us to have ya here, but the rumor is they'll be organizing a home guard which will seek out and arrest those who shirk their patriotic duties," she said gravely.

"Well, sweetheart," Immanuel began, "We ain't 'bout to shirk nothin', we's a been talkin' and soon as we gets our bearings well, we're gonna go north and find yer pa and brothers."

"Whatever for?" she asked.

"Well, we ain't decided that just yet, but we both imagine that generals will need trackers, and folks who can move 'bout between both sides and such," Immanuel said, taking a long puff on his pipe and blowing the smoke into the fire.

"That would be dangerous," Sally noted.

"No more so than fightin' Injuns and such," Uzziah threw his two cents in.

"Ya still fightin' Injuns out west?" she asked.

"Yep," Uzziah said and left it at that.

"I imagine that either the North or the South will use old grudges and get Injuns to help them track and fight," Immanuel said.

"But most Injuns around here are peaceful," Sally objected.

"Well, nothing like a nation torn apart by war to bring the old grudges out, is there, Uzziah?"

"Reckon not," he said, tapping out the dottle from his pipe and tossing it into the fire.

"Mama's got some whiskey hidden, and I know where it's at," Sally said, grinning.

"Well, well, brother Uzziah, didn't know ya had a sister who entertained such ideas," Immanuel said, licking his lips.

"Ya want some?" Sally asked.

Both the mountain men chuckled softly. "'Course we do, darlin'," Immanuel said.

Sally disappeared into the kitchen, and neither man could see where the bottle came from, and Uzziah figured that was good. It was a bottle of Jameson, his pa Sean's favorite, nothing like Irish whiskey. The bottle was nearly full, and Uzziah certainly hoped that it could be returned to its hiding place in nearly the same condition. She had three short glasses gathered with her fingers, guess they weren't the only ones who wanted a nip.

She set the glasses on the table between the rockers, the one with the lamp on it, and she poured three healthy shots.

"Who taught ya to pour, girl?" Immanuel asked.

"Pa a course," she said as she handed the men their glasses and raised hers.

"To the South, may it fight hard and win against the aggressors of the North!" and then she held out her glass for them to clink with hers. They did so, then all three threw back the shots.

Sally broke into a cough, which Immanuel helped her with by pounding her gently on the back.

"Sorry, didn't mean to seem like such a wimp," she apologized.

"Did ya and that boy stay together?" Uzziah asked her as she regained her composure and poured them three new shots, which she took a sip from.

"The boy's name is Frank Cummins, and we were married last time ya was chere," she said.

"That's right, ya moved to Harper's Ferry, didn't ya?" Uzziah asked.

"Yes, we did, yes," she said, remembering.

"No children?" Immanuel asked. "Why with hips like those, ya should have a passel of 'em by now!"

Sally downed the rest of her shot and looked at the two men, there were tears in her eyes.

"What'd I say?" Immanuel asked.

Sally reached out and took hold of Immanuel's arm.

"Nothin' darlin' ya just asked what anyone would ask," she said, then poured herself another shot, and the men, too.

"What happened to Bonnie?" Uzziah asked, and Sally burst into tears and went into Immanuel's arms. She sobbed uncontrollably, while Immanuel looked at his partner of all these years, wondering what was going on.

Suddenly, Sally broke from the sobbing hug, her cheeks stained with tears, "This is simply awful of me, mother will never forgive me. I am so sorry to have acted thusly," she said, pouring herself another shot.

"When did Bonnie die?" Uzziah asked, taking one of her hands in his.

Sally looked at her older brother and smiled a terribly sad smile. "Last year, scarlet fever got her. She was only four years old. We brought her down from up north and buried her out back in the family cemetery."

"Oh, darlin'," Uzziah said, and Sally smiled again with tears running down her cheeks.

"That ain't nothin', that Cummins boy, Frank, he loves the bottle now and not me. I left his sorry arse up there in Harpers Ferry to drink himself to death without an audience."

"Serves him right, darlin', he don't deserve ya," Immanuel said.

Sally looked at Immanuel and smiled a really nice smile, "Will ya marry me, Immanuel?" she whispered.

Both men froze there by the fire, sitting in their rockers, rocking no more, and Sally sitting on the milking stool with her bedclothes wrapped about her knees.

Immanuel looked at Uzziah, and Uzziah just looked back. What was there to say?

"Never mind, didn't mean it," Sally said, twirling her golden hair between her fingers, and finishing off the last shot she had poured, then she picked up the bottle and drank directly from it, gulping a bit, then through her whiskey-coated voice she whispered again, "I hope the Yankees kill his drunk arse." Then she rose before either man could react, and was up the stairs before they spoke.

"That poor child," Immanuel managed, pouring himself another shot.

"She's nearly thirty, partner," Uzziah commented.

"Ya think she meant it?" Immanuel asked.

"Which one, the proposal of marriage, or her husband's death wish?" Uzziah let out.

"Good point, good point. So, yer brothers and pa have gone north to join up, and Obadiah run off God knows where, what's we gonna do?"

"The only thing we can. We gots to find Obadiah and bring him back home," Uzziah said.

"He could be anywheres," Immanuel objected.

"I know where he is," Uzziah said.

"How?"

"He's my brother, fool, 'member he hid us in the caves when the Pinkertons were after us?"

"Yeah, I remember, but Sally said she went up there and there was no sign of 'em."

"Well, he ain't exactly a soldier, but he knows how to hide from his sister," Uzziah admitted.

"Being dumb never stopped nobody from fightin'," Immanuel remarked.

"Ya know this from experience, is that right?"

Immanuel stood up from his rocking chair and bowed up.

"I don't care ifn this is yourn house, home, whatever, I will kick yer butt, right here and now!"

"Sit down, old man."

"Who ya callin' old?" Immanuel said, punching the air as if he was just waiting for Uzziah to stand up.

"Ya haven't had that much to drink, have ya?" Uzziah asked.

"Nah!" Immanuel said and sat back down, then added, "But where'd she put the dang bottle?"

"It's right there," Uzziah said, pointing beside the milking stool Sally was sitting on, "but remember, she don't like drunks?"

"So...ya think she meant that, 'bout marrying me?"

"She could do worse, and so could ya, but that's not the question of the hour, is it?"

"No, guess not."

"We gots to go see ifn Obadiah made his way to the Confederate armies, and that's all there is to it."

"Ya think? Really?"

"My family has welcomed ya as a member, Obadiah helped hide us from that awful Pinkerton woman, it's the very least we can do," Uzziah said, and picked up the bottle and handed it to Immanuel.

"Don't mind if I do," he said and poured them both another shot.

They raised their glasses to each other and drank.

"But just remember, I'm a doin' this under protest," Immanuel said.

The men decided to sleep down there by the comforting fire, even though it wasn't that cold outside. The comforts of home are rarely forgotten, even when we grow older and have been gone for years. To Immanuel, it may not have seemed like such a blessing, but to Uzziah, he was transported back to his childhood, when the house only had one story, and his pa, Sean, had built the upper story one spring. He had helped, if you could call it that, bringing square-headed nails to the bucket that his father would pull up with the rope.

He had thought himself a big boy then, but he was just a boy. A little boy. His ma was already pregnant with his brother, Hank, and she helped, too, when she could. Hank was born before the addition to the home was finished, and by winter, it was all done except for the finer details, which Sean was so good at. And all the while, he tilled the soil, planted the seed, saw to the care and feeding of the livestock, and even managed to play his guitar and banjo from time to time, and they would all sing together the hymns and songs which they knew.

Growing up there at the farm had been ideal, wonderful, amazing, and it was at that moment that he realized why he left. For him, it had been too easy. There was no challenge in doing what a growing boy knew was his duty. There was no effort in being good, doing your chores, and helping younger siblings with theirs. It had been a blessing to be so raised up. And he knew it.

The day he came into the kitchen and told his mother he was leaving, it was as if she had been waiting, waiting for him to come around. Supporting children was one thing, but he had been nearly twenty when he left, and it was time. Neither his ma, Rahab, nor his pa, Sean, had objected in the least. And in a manner of speaking, it made him feel that he might have been tardy in his leaving, tardy in his realization that it was time for him to make his own way.

Of course, when he told them of the Rocky Mountains and the life he expected to lead, well, that was different. They had expected him to get a job in one of the surrounding towns to save and buy his own spread, or maybe marry into other lands, or anything but going on the other side of the moon. Rahab especially had been crushed. He was her favorite and always would be —of course, she would never say that to the others—but the news of him leaving and going, going, going so far away had taken her breath away.

As an older man, he knew all this now, he and his ma had talked it through the last time he had been there, and she was actually glad that what he had done had changed him into something that he would not have been changed into if he had stayed in the valley. The move to the mountains, his association, and eventual friendship with Immanuel had grown the boy into an unlikely man, and she marveled at it.

They had had time, earlier in the day, for him to tell her about his Mormon wife, Hannah, and the child that had barely lived, and how when he and Immanuel had taken those Mormons under Brigham Young's care west, and his friendship with the inimitable Porter Rockwell, well, her head was spinning. She had asked him, "Are ya still a Mormon, son?"

He had answered the only way he knew how, that he was celestial married to Hannah and that in heaven she was waiting for him.

"But does that make ya a Mormon?" she had asked, concerned. He wasn't sure why.

"It makes me a faithful husband. That's what it makes me," he had replied, and the subject was dropped.

"Look, Ma, it's the same Jesus, no matter what. Remember in scripture when the disciples came and said there were others in another country preaching his name? What did Jesus say?" Uzziah had asked his ma.

"That if they weren't again us, they were fer us," she had replied, proud that her upbringing had kept the boy so close to the Word of God, and that automatically kept him close to Jesus, since it said right there in the beginning of John, *In the beginning there was the word, and the word was with God, and the word was God. The same was in the beginning with God, and not anything that was made was made without him.*

Sometime in the night, he knew what they must do.

He and Immanuel must ride north toward Winchester and find the Confederate army. It was rumored to be led under Confederate General Joseph E. Johnston. They would find the general's camp and ask about their family, well, his family, but whatever he was related to, well, so was his partner, Immanuel.

5

The plans were further explained to Immanuel before anyone came down, then at the breakfast table, where country ham, fried apples, and grits and eggs were served, Uzziah told the entire group of women. They had reacted as he knew they would, sorry to lose his companionship and the protection that two mountain men offered, but glad that their brothers, especially Obadiah and father, would be looked for and perhaps be surrounded with the blessings which the two partners had enjoyed all these years.

"Are ya gonna put on the gray and fight fer the South?" Hanna asked, sure that they would.

"Well, no, we know from what we've heard already that those big ole armies need scouts. We'll join in with whatever group Pa has decided to join up with, and scout for them," Uzziah had said.

"I wish I could join. I'd like to kill me some Yankees," Hanna said. And everyone at the table knew that she meant it. *She could shoot as straight as any man, and if her hair had been cropped and enough clothes thrown over her body, no one would ever know*, Uzziah thought. He shook his head and silently cursed himself for even thinking such a thought.

They said their goodbyes, and mounting up on Shadow and Stygian, they trotted off down the farm road toward the main one. The women, all of them, stood on the porch and watched them ride until they all went up on the widow's walk and watched until their shapes were indistinguishable dots on the horizon. Their love and prayers went with them, and no one had spoken until they were totally out of sight.

The two mountain men had known, at least Uzziah had known, or felt in his gut that Joe Johnston would no longer be at Harpers Ferry. After relieving Colonel Thomas Jonathon Jackson at Harpers Ferry, Johnston did not like the fact that the town of Harpers Ferry was situated in a bowl of sorts and vulnerable to attack all around. It was then that he moved all his troops. These troops, now known as the Army of the Shenandoah, retreated to Winchester, Virginia. Johnston's continual use of strategic retreats would eventually earn him the sobriquet of *Retreatin' Joe* or *the Great Retreater*.

Two days later, when Uzziah and Immanuel reached Winchester, Virginia, the sleepy little hamlet had been changed into a bustling army camp. Excitement was in the air, and a great relief surrounded the town since now it was impregnable to attack from the northern aggressors.

"Damn!" Immanuel spoke as they rode easily down

the main street of Winchester. "These people seem thrilled that the Confederate army is chere!"

"Yeah, there's a certain feelin' 'bout the place, that's a fer sure," Uzziah answered.

"So, what's our next move? Ya guessed right about 'em being chere, but how in the hell do we find the needles in this chere haystack?"

"There's got to be 12,000 men here ifn there's a dozen," Uzziah agreed.

It was then that they saw an officer riding his horse down the street. Uzziah pulled Shadow over toward the officer and held his hand up in greeting.

"Yes, sir, how can I be of help?" the captain said in a strong Virginia accent.

"Where would the commander of all this be at this very moment?" Uzziah asked.

The captain was no fool, and he knew that the Confederacy would be in need of scouts, and these two mountain men might just be the thing.

"Please do me the honor of letting me escort you both to General Joseph Johnston," the captain said.

"Thank ya, sir!" Uzziah replied, having no idea what the captain had in mind.

As they moved through the mass of Confederate soldiers who were dressed in homespun clothes, some of them gray but the majority of them homespun ochres, yellows, and browns. The men looked like they had left their fields and grabbed rifles, which, in essence, was exactly what the majority of them had done.

Unfortunately, for the North, most of those in good blue uniforms were either drafted when they arrived off boats from Ireland, due to the potato famine, or simply city men, who had abandoned the ways of their forebearers.

The South may have had fewer men, but their marksmanship was not a matter of pride, but rather the manner in which meat was put on the table. Wasting shot was not in their bones, and hitting the targets they aimed at was, be they wild deer or bluebellies.

Finally, the captain pulled up near an important-looking tent. An adjutant came over.

"Can I help you, Captain?"

"Yes, I would like to speak to General Johnston."

The adjutant disappeared into the tent and moments later came back out.

"General Johnston will see you," he said.

"Dismount and wait here," the captain said as he disappeared into the tent. They did as they were ordered, and as they waited, Uzziah noticed the tent flap momentarily opened, then re-shut. It was not the captain, but an older man, possible in his late forties, balding, and in uniform. Uzziah figured that must have been the general.

Fairly soon, after that, the adjutant who had spoken to the captain came out.

"The general will see you now," he said. Both the partners looked at each other and, guessing their quandary, the adjutant took their reins from them.

"Thank ye," Immanuel said, and the two men walked to the tent, pulled back the flap, and ducked inside.

Outside, the day had been bright, and coming within the confines of the large tent, their eyes took a moment to readjust. When they could properly see again, they were being stared at by an older man—the same one who had spied on them from the tent—as he was seated behind a field table.

"The captain here," he said, indicating the man standing to one side of the table with his revolver removed from its holster and held in front of him, "said you wished to speak to me."

Uzziah spoke first, although he wasn't sure that was what Immanuel wanted, but that's the way it happened.

"Sir!" Uzziah said, and he saluted the general, and that got a smile from Johnston, "I am Uzziah Ferguson O'Bannon, and this is my partner, Immanuel James Jones. We have recently returned from the Rockies and wish to serve as scouts for the general."

Immanuel's head whipped to look at Uzziah, who kept looking at General Johnston.

"I take it this may not be your wish, Mr. Jones?" the general asked.

"Ah, no sir, it's just we hadn't exactly discussed how we was gonna go 'bout this, and I'm a bit surprised."

"Don't you wish to scout for my army?" Johnston asked.

Immanuel made a futile attempt at a salute, which made the general smile, then he spoke, "Sir, whatever Uzziah has said goes equally fer me, we're partners, ya see."

"Loyalty, as you might imagine, I find that a good trait in my men," Johnston said, then added, "I take it by the fact that both of you looked seasoned"—which was a nice way of saying that probably he had smelled them before he saw them—"and the fact that both have your topknots, that you know what you're doing?"

"We do, sir, we have been caught in some tight

spots, and we still do have our hair!" Immanuel proudly spoke.

This got a chuckle from both the captain and the general.

"Well," continued the general, "I was a civilian in the second of the Florida wars against the Seminoles and at Jupiter Florida we had gone ashore and were attacked by no less than thirty of the savages. This scar," he said, putting his finger to his scalp where there was a white scar, "I received that day along with no less than a dozen bullet holes in my clothing. I'm not sure how I survived, but survive I did. I have the utmost respect for men such as yerselves. Are either of you from Virginia?"

"Yes, sir, my family has a large farm in the middle of the valley."

"That's really why we're here," Immanuel continued.

"Yeah, yeah, that's right," Uzziah continued, "my pa and my six brothers, I think they might be with your troops,"

"And they're all O'Bannons?" Johnston asked.

"Yes, sir," Uzziah said, impressed that the general had remembered his name.

"What do you think, Captain? Can we help these gentlemen?"

"Yes, sir, I think we can."

"Very good then, Captain Willis will take you around the encampment. You'll find it's rather organized, even though there are so many, but first I must ask you both a question," the general said.

"Yes, sir," both answered at the same time, and that brought another smile to Johnston's face.

"Will you both scout for us?"

The two partners looked at each other and smiled, but Immanuel's smile was wryer than Uzziah's.

"Yes, sir, as long as I've located my kin, we both will be glad to," Uzziah said.

"One last thing," Johnston said. "Scouts are never in uniform, just dress the way you dress, but if caught, they will hang you as spies, which, of course, you will be."

"I'd rather face the prospect of a noose over a silent flying arrow," Uzziah said.

"As would I," Johnston said.

Uzziah saluted the general.

"And do not salute me again, you are scouts and as such it is not required," the general said.

The smell of shite was everywhere as they meandered through the rows of tents. As the general had commented, they may all be Virginians without so much as being dressed alike, but the tents which the Confederacy had supplied them were fairly uniform. Row upon row of tents and men going about their business. Some were on the parade grounds, as they called it, an open space where men with their rifles could drill, marching up and down and listening to the commands of their superiors.

"As you can imagine, if this weren't done," the captain started in, "all hell would break loose when the fighting begins. And it will begin."

"Are the Yankees comin' this way?" Immanuel asked.

"No, sir, not yet, as best we can tell, and this is

based on intelligence we received this morning, they are amassing outside Washington, and camped there, like they're afraid we are going to attack," Captain Willis said.

"When do ya think they'll attack and how will we know?" Uzziah asked.

"Well, we're far enough away that that won't happen. We won't be attacked here, but most likely they will eventually advance, and when that happens, a courier will be sent our way."

They had continued to ride up and down the columns of tents, and Uzziah was looking at the horses as well as the men.

"But that there in Washington—how many miles is that, Uzziah?" Immanuel asked.

"It's three days by good horse," Uzziah commented as he continued to watch for his pa and brothers.

"Well, Johnston's got an ace up his sleeve when it comes to getting to the battle," Captain Willis said.

"We gonna take the train?" Immanuel joked.

"Precisely," Captain Willis said.

The mountain men looked incredulously at each other. Whatever else was happening, this new war was going to be fought like no other war had ever been fought—taking the train to a battle, whoever heard of such a thing?

Uzziah thought he would spot his family, but Captain Willis knew that it was much more likely that the two mountain men would be spotted by the O'Bannon family before they were. And that was the way it happened.

"Hey, hey! Uzziah! Brother Uzziah, over chere!" came a cry from three rows over, and when Uzziah looked, who should be jumping up and down but Obadiah, his cave-dwelling brother!

Before they could even start in that direction, Obadiah was jumping and running through the rows of tents.

Then, he was there, hugging Uzziah's leg and looking up at him as if a part of home had made it all the way to Winchester, Virginia.

"Where's everybody?" Uzziah asked.

"They's marching and moving to commands. I was sick this morning and stayed behind."

Uzziah grabbed Obadiah's arm and pulled him up behind him on Shadow and kicked the horse up toward the parade grounds.

Immanuel was right behind them, as was the captain. When they got to the marching soldiers, Uzziah recognized Raymond's raven hair before anything else. Marching with him were Hank, Short Samson, Zachariah, John, and, not seeing their pa, Sean, he heard his pa's voice giving the commands. How in the heck did Sean know how to march troops?

"Do not ride onto the parade grounds, Uzziah!" That command came from Captain Willis, and they all rode their horses to the edge of what looked like a large green square.

Uzziah could tell that all his brothers had seen them now, but their marching orders were coming from their pa, Sean, who was now even sterner. Sean O'Bannon obviously wanted the officers on the field to know that he could command the troops no matter what the circumstance. After all, he wanted to keep his sons together, in the same rifle squad under his leadership. The only way to do that was to show his prowess in leading the men he had fathered.

There was a verbal command from one of the officers watching the marching, and that brought the company to a halt. Each company was made up of several platoons, each platoon of four squads. Other orders were shouted out at the company level, then passed on by platoon leaders. It was easy to visualize the notion of a chain of command when verbal orders rolled down that chain. Then the command, "Dismissed," came from the captain in charge of the company, and the men broke formation, while the brothers O'Bannon and their pa, Sean, ran toward the edge of the field where Uzziah, Immanuel, and Captain Willis waited.

6

Uzziah and Immanuel sat around the campfire where the sons of Sean O'Bannon had gathered. At that point in the war, commanders were willing, more or less, to accommodate families, as long as families accommodated the army. That is, when seven men showed, and one was the pa, and the other the sons, they let that be and trained around it. They, the Confederate elite, knew that men would defend their own kin with a dying passion. Of course, Sean secretly wished that they could have avoided all this, but when Virginia succeeded, what could he do? His boys, especially the youngest, John, were ready to go the minute it happened. There was no talking him or the others out of it. Once the youngest had committed himself, the others were obliged, more or less, to follow suit.

Sean was amazed that Uzziah had shown up, and even more amazed that his partner had followed him into this mess. Everyone thought the war would last maybe a month, or two, but Sean knew, just by looking at what the Confederacy had gathered together—thanks to the arsenals which were in every state, and the fact that men of the South lived with guns, it was just a fact, that there was no quit in these southern boys and the Union thinking that there was, would prepare that same Union for many disappointments.

"Pa, what do ya think?" It was Uzziah, and to tell the truth, Sean had no idea what they were talking about.

"Sorry, son, I was lost in thought," Sean said.

"Thinkin' 'bout Ma?" Uzziah asked.

"No, honestly, that woman could take care of all of us, if we let her," Sean said, and the other brothers sitting around finishing up the meal that Uzziah had cooked, and it was a damned good one, laughed, and elbows were being thrown into ribs.

"Pa, yer just sayin' that, right?" It was Obadiah, and he was serious. He thought the world of his mother, but having come along instead of hiding in one of his caves or staying with the womenfolk, he wanted his pa to be strong.

"Pa ain't no fool, Obie, ifn he says something agin ma here, it will surely get back into the valley," Raymond said, and everyone had a good laugh.

The camaraderie continued for the evening, but when taps were played, and even Uzziah knew what that meant, it was time for the troops to turn in. Both Uzziah and Immanuel were given invitations to tents, but the two mountain men were so used to sleeping outdoors that it seemed more unnatural to go into a tent than to simply throw down your saddle and roll out your bedroll.

The fire was dying down, and both mountain men

were awake, looking at the rising waxing crescent as it came up over Winchester, when Immanuel spoke up.

"Young son, what have ya done to us?" he asked sotto vice.

"Whatcha talking 'bout?" Uzziah asked.

"Back there in the general's tent..." Immanuel started, then trailed off.

"Yeah, what 'bout it?"

"Ya basically volunteered us into the fight!" Immanuel whispered, but it was a desperate whisper.

"Well, I just thought—"

"What'd ya think! I ain't no damned Virginian, hell, half of me's Mandan and the other half hails from Baltimore, and I don't imagine they's gonna fight fer no Confederacy."

"Well, I just thought—"

"Ya didn't think, young son, ya didn't!"

"Well, what do ya wanna do?" Uzziah asked sincerely.

"It's a little late fer that, don't ya think? Like asking a woman ifn she wants to bed ya, after ya done stuck it in!"

"I had no idea, really!"

"I know, I wish I didn't feel this way, young son, but..." he trailed off.

"Ya can go back, ya know," Uzziah sort of asked and sort of stated.

"No, Uzziah, I can't, not now. I done trained you up, and yer mine as far as yer skills go, and these young boys who are all so fired up, and their breasts swellin' with the honor of the fight, hell, young son, they don't have the slightest idea what's goin' on, and ya know it!"

The two men sat there, on their bedrolls, the glow

of the fire in their faces. Uzziah thought about how many times his life had been saved by the older man, he thought about how many times he had saved Immanuel's life. And in that instance, he realized that Immanuel was right. He had been taught in the school of mountainmanship, and what was about to happen between the North and the South, well, that was sheer slaughter, and both the partners knew it.

It was family that had gotten him to this point, and Uzziah knew that family and this strange obligation and love for his state of Virginia. Family was everything, then he thought about his partner and how he had been raised, how the man had literally as a teenager, sacrificed himself for his blood relatives, his ma, and his brothers, how he'd been taken by the Sioux and then escaped, and how all this had been locked up in his mind, till that fateful day, when he thought the end of his life was near and he fessed up.

If those Pawnees hadn't been there, and the sureness of death hadn't been in the air, the man would never have confessed his fears, and once they were away from the danger, he was hard pressed to do anything about it. What the hell had Uzziah done?!? Once again, it was a perfect example of him thinking that Immanuel's thoughts and his thoughts were the same, and how many times had he found that that simply was not the case?!?

"I am sincerely sorry, my friend, I thought that we were of one mind on this, and I didn't bother to check in with ya," Uzziah said, then added, "We can go back to the mountains, we can."

Immanuel just looked at his partner and smiled. The boy, well, he was a man now, but he meant well.

Immanuel knew Uzziah loved his family and his state, Ole Dominion, he called it. Immanuel had no illusions about states and states' rights. He thought of himself as simply a mountain man, a man from the Rockies. But he had, in more ways than one, attached himself to this Virginian. And yes, they were partners, but there was something else which had been percolating between them, something familial, something son/father like, something that bridged gaps that he thought could, would never be spanned.

The man had become a Mormon, met Joseph Smith and Porter Rockwell, married Hannah and had a child, and they had taken her remains out to the cabins and buried them in the high meadow, and he, Immanuel, knew that Uzziah would never marry again, even though it wasn't because he believed in that celestial marriage crap. What he believed in was what Uzziah believed. And the young man could not be faulted for falling both in love and in wonder with the prophets from the LDS.

Immanuel's gods had been in lesser ones, alcohol, gambling, and women, not necessarily in that order, and they had played hell with him, leaving him literally heartbroken and wasted. Leaving him yearning only to get back to his mountains and be with the younger man that he considered–what did he consider Uzziah? Something which could not be put into words, something that defied speech, something almost spiritual, well, at least what he considered spiritual.

"Whatcha wanna do, partner, I'll do whatever, promise, ya mean a whole bunch to me." It was Uzziah who had interrupted Immanuel's thoughts, and now, as the older man looked at his younger partner, a warm feeling grew up inside of this older father figure. He knew that if he left and Uzziah was killed, he would never forgive himself, but what the hell!

"We're stayin', and ya know it. Damn ya kid, I'd do anything fer ya, and ya know that, too," Immanuel said and looked away a bit embarrassed by the admission.

"Immanuel, we don't—"

"Shut yer piehole, we're stayin'," Immanuel said, and he turned his back on his partner of many years and curled into his blankets. That was a universal sign between the two of them that whatever was going on was going on no longer.

Uzziah smiled at Immanuel's back. He knew how the older man felt about him, and he knew the older man knew how he felt about him. They were partners. That might not mean a lot to some people, but in the mountains where death was surety and partners were more than just two men who rode together, they were the guarantee that their riding would maybe not end in a terrible death. When men took those vows of partnership, well, it was a physical bond, as physical as the air that existed between them. Uzziah smiled again and rolled into his bedroll, satisfied that the discussion was over—for now.

Taps had been something nice when lights went out, something novel, but it seemed as if the bugler who awakened the camp that morning was standing awfully close to where the two partners slept, well, had slept.

Both mountain men were amazed at how quickly the *troops* had shaken themselves out of their bunks, and prepared their meals, and were ready for another day in the Confederate army, more marching, more orders, more army stuff.

But this particular day was an exception. General Joseph E. Johnston had received orders that he should move his troops from Winchester to Manassas, Virginia. The first battle of the Civil War was looming like a bad moon rising on the horizon.

General Winfield Scott, who had led troops, and the generals who were now about to fight this war, warned President Abraham Lincoln not to attack too early. The troops which had been conscripted from the various northern states were not ready, they were not an army, but a mob all dressed the same. And yet, the battle cry of *On to Richmond* had been exclaimed so many times in the streets of Washington that political pressure had made the final decision for Lincoln beyond his and the general's misgivings.

As early as the 16th of July, crowds had run along General McDowell's carriage as it made its way down the streets of Washington, all shouting that he should go *On to Richmond*!

The Union was so confident in their immediate victory that carriages full of bystanders had followed General McDowell's troops out of Washington with their cheeses and wine, all set for an interesting outing in which the rebellion would be put down for good.

The Confederate troops in Winchester, meantime, were formed up on the 21st of July, and since neither Uzziah nor Immanuel belonged to any regiment or company, they rode up front with the general. They were, after all, scouts, a different breed, with the army, but not of it. Their objective was the Piedmont Station, where they would board trains that would take them to Manassas, Virginia.

The fact that this was the first time that such rails were used in the United States in transporting troops to a war was lost on just about everybody. All they knew and were heartily glad for was the fact that they wouldn't be marching all the way to Manassas. Johnston knew different, the train ride would give them the illusion of safety, then they would be pushed out into the first real battle, and only God knew what that might mean for them.

For Immanuel and Uzziah, who had spent so many years away from crowds, the sight of 12,000 men on foot marching in some sort of order was an amazing thing to see and hear. In fact, it was downright disconcerting. The clanging of their equipment, their canteens, muskets, bayonets, and other army gear made a most distinctive sound, which, when listened to long enough, could have put a person to sleep. The machine of war had its own rhythm.

"Scouts!" General Johnston yelled.

Both Immanuel and Uzziah rode up alongside the general.

"Yes, sir?" Uzziah said.

"Piedmont Station is not that far ahead. I would like it if you could scout on ahead and make sure that no Union troops have not surreptitiously occupied Piedmont Station and that the train is ready for this loading," General Johnston said, and Uzziah started to salute, but didn't.

"Yes, sir," Uzziah said, and two magnificent black horses took off down the road in front of the troops.

"No matter what you say, those two mountain men

have excellent taste in horseflesh," the general said to his adjutant.

"Yes, sir, they do. The older one—"

"Immanuel?"

"Yes, sir, he rides Stygian, and he told me he'd purchased the horse at a New Orleans racetrack."

"A thoroughbred, huh? What about the other black?"

"Uzziah's horse, well, I never found out where he got it, but it's rumored that they can outrace anyone following them," the Lieutenant said.

"Good thing to have in Indian territory," Johnston said, and that was the end of the discussion.

Uzziah and Immanuel were holding to a good lope, riding their blacks as if they were riding the wind.

"Glad ya knew what the general was saying," Immanuel said.

"Whatcha mean?"

"Ain't never heard that word, what was it, surreptitiously?"

"Just means secretly," Uzziah explained.

"Why people use $1.50 words when a 25-cent word would do? Just don't understand that."

"Vocabulary isn't something they do on purpose," Uzziah tried to explain.

"What the hell's *vocabulary*?"

"Never mind," Uzziah said as they rode on.

They made good time as they traveled down the road toward Piedmont Station. Fairly soon, well, within the hour, the town came into view. They decided it was the better part of valor to circle the town and look for Union troops. There didn't seem to be any troops in sight, so they rode to the train station, and Immanuel held Uzziah's reins as he jumped off Shadow and walked to the ticket window.

"Is there a train here for General Johnston's troops?"

The ticket master looked up and was surprised to see someone dressed like they were an Injun.

"Who the hell wants to know?"

"We scout for the general," Uzziah said.

"Sure ya do, got any proof?"

"Well, what kinda proof would that be? A badge saying I'm a scout?"

"Yeah, well, that kinda makes sense, I guess," the ticket master said, then added, "See those passenger and boxcars over there on the siding?"

Uzziah looked, and there were a lot of passenger cars and some boxcars used for transporting stock sitting on the siding.

"Those there?" he asked, pointing.

"That's them, and ifn ya ain't a Yankee spy, that's what ya'll be riding, son," the ticket master said.

Uzziah walked to the edge of the depot, and Immanuel held out his reins. He mounted up, and they high-tailed it back up the Piedmont Station Road.

By the time they had made it almost back to the column of marching men, there came a rousing song which neither Immanuel nor Uzziah had heard before. As they got closer, they began to hear the lyrics clearly, and from the way it sounded, it would be the national anthem of the South. The marching boys were singing lustily. Uzziah didn't know whose idea that was, but it sounded good, twelve thousand voices raised in song.

"I wish I was in the land of cotton, Old times there are not forgotten!

"Look away! Look away! Look away! Dixie Land!

"In Dixie Land where I was born in, early on one frosty morning,

"Look away! Look away! Look away! Dixie Land!

"Then I wish I was in Dixie! Hooray! Hooray!

"In Dixie Land I'll take my strand, to live and die in Dixie!

"Away! Away! Away down South in Dixie!

"Away! Away! Away down South in Dixie!"

Uzziah and Immanuel rode up alongside a smiling Joseph E. Johnston.

"I sure hope there aren't Federal troops at Piedmont Station, hell, they'll hear us miles before we get there," the general said, smiling all the while.

"No, General, there's only trains and regular people at the station," Uzziah said.

"Well, good, maybe we'll get a turnout to see the boys off," Johnston remarked.

And they did. By the time the column of fighting men had made the town, the town was lined up on either side of the main street that led to the depot. They had sung the song so many times that some of the boys were hoarse, but that didn't stop their grinning voices from singing out as they reached the depot.

"I wish I was in the land of cotton, Old times there are not forgotten!

"Look away! Look away! Look away! Dixie Land!

"In Dixie Land where I was born in, early on one frosty morning,

"Look away! Look away! Look away! Dixie Land!"

Several townspeople who played in a small band had gathered at the depot, and they joined in. It was rousing as the troops single-filed their way onto the passenger cars, and the singing and the band continued. One young lady ran out and hugged a soldier, and that prompted several others to do the same. Some of the women handed soldiers their scarves and other knickknacks.

"And people wonder why man goes to war?" Johnston remarked.

It was true this rabble-rousing time, the song, the band music, it all joined together to do something to one's spirit. Even Immanuel was singing along on Stygian as he made his way to the stockcars, and he was rewarded by a woman who ran over. He leaned down, and she kissed him on the cheek and gave him her kerchief, which he tied about his neck.

Once they had loaded their horses on the stockcars, it was obvious to both mountain men that all Johnston's troops were not going to fit on this particular train. The officers under Johnston loaded as many as possible, and the others were left with their company commanders at Piedmont Station for the train that would return and pick them up.

There was so much happening that Uzziah lost track of his pa and brothers as the train loaded up. They both took their horses, along with the officers who were with the troops, to the stockcars, and they were loaded up and tended to. Once that was done, they walked the long line of passenger cars where the singing had finally died down and the excited chatter of boys going off to war filled the air.

"Uzziah! Uzziah! Over here!" It was Obadiah shouting as he leaned out the window of one of the passenger cars. "We saved ya seats!"

They got on that car, and everyone was so excited, and sure enough, there were two seats right there beside Uzziah's pa.

Immanuel took their gear and stowed it in the wooden bins overhead. Then the train jerked once, and a mighty, excited shout went up from 12,000 voices. The train rocked again, and again another shout, and then slowly the train started out for good toward their destination, Manassas Station.

Uzziah looked at his six brothers, they were all either eating something they had brought along from breakfast or chatting with one another. He couldn't help but think that if this war continued, they probably all wouldn't make it without being scathed. He didn't wish to think about death, but that's what happened in wars, domestic or foreign. One army wins by killing more of the opposing army. That was the mantra of war.

Several of his brothers caught him staring at them, but Uzziah simply smiled, and they would continue with what they were doing. He was glad his mother, Rahab, wasn't here and that his sisters were back at the farm out of harm's way. But he did realize that if this conflict did not resolve itself quickly, the Shenandoah Valley would be important for both the South to maintain succoring its troops or the Union to cut those supplies off and steal them for their own Federal troops.

The chatter and excitement went from a lot of talking to nearly silence as they finished up the thirty-four miles to Manassas Station.

On the 18th of July, three days earlier, General McDowell's army, 35,000 strong, had reached Centerville. Five miles ahead of him, there ran a stream named Bull Run. And guarding all the fords of that stream from Union Mills to the Stone Bridge was General Pierre G.T. Beauregard, who waited with 22,000 troops.

7

By noon on the 21st of July, Johnston had finally gotten all his men off the trains, and with Beauregard, they had reached the area at Henry Hill where they would support Jackson's 1st Virginia Brigade.

For an hour and a half, they sat back in the woods as they were bombarded by the Federal cannons. Men who would never get a chance to fight for their beloved Virginia were being blown up. Marching all that way, riding the trains and all, and now only to be blown to bits.

Uzziah and Immanuel had seen where the vast majority of shells were falling, and sizing up the range of the cannons, they moved the O'Bannon family forward close to the front of the woods. Nothing seemed to be falling there.

The noise was unbelievable, no one had ever heard such sounds. The shells exploding, the Confederate cannons rolling back down the slight incline and out of sight of the Yankee muskets and rifled cannons, as they were reloaded, pushed back up, and fired again. This seemed to go on for an eternity.

Uzziah was watching something else that had captured his imagination. General Thomas Jonathan Jackson, still dressed in his blue Virginia Military Institute uniform, was riding a smallish roan mare up and down the line of men who were gathered in the woods. Minie ball rifle shots were whizzing by him and his horse, and all he did the entire time was to ride slowly up and down the line.

"Steady, men, steady. All's well." That was his watchword as he rode up and down the line. At one point, he rode up closer to the cannons to get a better look at what was happening along the Yankee line, and sharpshooters all down that observed Yankee line were homing in their aim on him. Still, he sat there looking through his binoculars.

An officer in his command rode up and while Jackson was talking to him, he, Jackson, had raised his left arm—Uzziah found out later that it was that particular arm which Jackson felt had always weighed more than his right arm and raising it above his head relieved the pressure of the heavy arm—and at that very moment a Minie ball grazed the middle finger on Jackson's left hand. The officer with Jackson made some comment concerning the hand, and Uzziah heard Jackson reply. "Only a scratch, a mere scratch," he said as he took his handkerchief out and wrapped the hand.

"Uzziah, did ya see that?" It was Obadiah who had worked his way to where Uzziah was lying with his other brothers and men from Johnston's regiment.

"Yes, Obie, I did see it. He's one hell of a brave man," Uzziah said.

"I heard from some of the others that it ain't that, he prays every morning for three hours, and this being a Sunday, this is a sacred battle for him," Obadiah whispered to Uzziah.

Uzziah watched Jackson and the other officer till the officer rode away, but when he turned to Obadiah, he wasn't there.

"Uzziah, look, look!" It was Sean O'Bannon, their pa, who was yelling at Uzziah and pointing back toward where Jackson sat his horse.

In the confusion of the moment Obadiah had run through the hiding troops and was speaking something to Jackson who nodded his head, evidently in agreement, and then—the hell of it all—Obadiah knelt down in the middle of all those flying shells right there beside Jackson, and Jackson lifting his arms up, was praying for them as Obadiah bowed his head.

"What the hell?" It was Immanuel who was now beside Uzziah. "Should I go get him?"

"Nah, he's under God's protection now," Uzziah said, half meaning it, and half not.

It was at this moment in the battle that the Federals were rushing down Matthew's Hill, and General Bernard Bee, a South Carolinian with a big black mustache and a full head of black hair, rode up to Jackson, and in his excited state, everyone in the front lines could hear him.

Interrupting Jackson's prayer, evidently, General Bee shouted out excitedly, "General, they are driving us!!"

"Then, sir," Jackson shouted back over the thundering Confederate cannons and the exploding shells behind them, "we will give them the bayonet!"

Bee, not a fan of the bayonet, flew down the crest of the hill where officers of his retreating units were trying to piece together a resistance to the onslaught of Federals.

General Bee drew his sword and, pointing to the top of the hill where Jackson serenely sat his horse, boomed out in a loud voice, "Look, men, there is Jackson standing like a stone wall! Let us determine to die here, and we will conquer! Follow me!" he shouted and brandishing his sword he rode back up the hill followed by all those who had moments before been retreating.

What happened next was anybody's guess. Uzziah, sitting beside the campfire that night, tried to remember, but in the fog of war, his mind could not wrap itself around what exactly had happened. One thing was for sure, Jackson had held, and the Federals, surprised at the stiff resistance of what they thought was a retreating army, faltered, with many falling, and finally, they turned and retreated in anything but an orderly fashion.

Uzziah, Immanuel, and the brothers O'Bannon had run after the retreating Federals, and looking down the pike road, all Uzziah could see was a road choked with the retreating Federals and those who had come out from Washington with their picnic baskets to see the rebellion put down for good!

The sight was enough to enliven the most stalwart heart. The excitement with which he and his brothers had run after the retreating Federals, and the countless Union soldiers who had fallen in disgrace with bullet holes in their backs, well, this was war, and they were defending Virginia! Finally, the congestion down at the pike road, and the fact that most, if not all, the Union soldiers were throwing away their muskets and backpacks and running pall mall toward Washington, convinced Jackson to call a halt. Uzziah couldn't help but wonder what would have happened if they had followed those retreating well onto the streets of Washington. Perhaps the Federals had been right, and the Confederacy would have won the day, taken over the capital of the Union, and a peace would have been negotiated. And yet, that did not happen.

That night, the Confederate army camped on the same grounds where the battle had raged. The dead lay around, both Federal and Confederate, as supper was fixed. Uzziah was busy cooking for his kin.

He looked over at Obadiah and just had to say something. "Obie, come here," he said in his good brotherly voice. Obadiah got up and moved over to where Uzziah was cooking.

"Ya makin' biscuits?" Obadiah asked.

"Yeah, they're in the Dutch oven. Say, can ya explain something to me?"

"Sure, ifn I know, I will."

"What were ya doin' runnin' out there and speaking to Gen. Jackson, then kneeling by him?"

"Ya didn't see it?"

"Yes, I did, I saw ya run out regardless of harm to yerself and kneel down with the bullets flyin' all around."

"No, not that, ya didn't see the cloud of blessing surrounding him?" Obadiah asked. And Uzziah thought to himself, this was exactly why their ma,

Rahab, didn't want Obie out in this war, the reason she had tried so desperately to keep him at home.

"What ya mean *cloud of blessing*?"

"As he was sittin' there and the bullets were flyin' all around him, a cloud of blessin' descended over the general, just like the one which had follered the Israelites through the desert on their way to the Promised Land. He were under God's protection," Obadiah said, his face glowing in the remembrance of it.

"Well, I didn't see it. All I saw was ya being reckless and runnin' toward danger," Uzziah said.

"Weren't no danger, I was within the cloud, and so was Fancy."

"Who's Fancy?" Uzziah asked, not sure he wanted to know.

"General Jackson's hoss, he bought it fer his wife, but it's so steady, he decided to keep it fer himself," Obadiah said.

Sean O'Bannon came running up.

"We can't find John," he whispered to Uzziah as he squatted by the fire. Out behind his pa, Uzziah could see the bloated bodies of some of the fallen, both Union and Confederate.

"What ya mean ya can't find him?!?" Uzziah asked urgently.

"Just that. Ya think he ran away?" Sean asked.

"Not John, no," Uzziah said and looked over to Immanuel, who was smoking.

"Then..." Sean trailed off.

"Get the other boys over chere and eat, Immanuel and I will find him," Uzziah said.

As Sean O'Bannon gathered up the other five boys,

who all had survived the first battle of the Civil War, as it would be called, and they spooned portions, leaving enough for Uzziah, his partner, and their youngest brother. They ate excitedly as their oldest brother and his partner went in search of the youngest and dearest of them.

Both sides were lining up their dead and trying to sort things out. Uzziah remembered that they had been back in the woods before the advance on Henry Hill, so he and Immanuel got about ten feet apart and walked back into the woods, where there were plenty of dead, or parts of them, as they had been blown up by the Federal cannon barrage that had lasted nearly two hours.

"There ain't much of some of these boys left," Immanuel commented as both men had taken burning branches from the fire to torch their way.

At first, it looked to Uzziah as if John had been hiding and he had found him, and like back at the farm, John would jump up and run for the home base of the hiding game and scream out, *Ollie, ollie, oxen free!* and be safe. But then he realized that the eyes staring up at him were dull and had no vision. He knelt down beside the boy's body, the body of his youngest brother John, who had just turned seventeen, or was it August yet? No, he was still sixteen.

Immanuel noticed that Uzziah had knelt down and was not continuing in the search. He came over with his torch and beheld perhaps the saddest thing he had ever witnessed. The oldest of the O'Bannon brothers kneeling, as if in prayer, beside the perfectly untouched but dead body of his youngest brother, John. His body was untouched, and yet he was dead as dead could be. It had been the shock of the exploding shell which had concussed his brain and left him absolutely perfectly dead, as if the life had simply run from his body in fright, and who's to say it hadn't?

They both looked back to where John's other brothers and his pa were squatting around the campfire and eating. What were they to do, wait? No, of course not, Uzziah handed his Hawken, which was like an appendage of his body, to his partner, Immanuel, and picked up his youngest brother and shifting the weight in his arms. He didn't weigh hardly anything, then he began to walk to where his kin were eating supper.

As he made his way with Immanuel beside him, Uzziah couldn't help but think of all his brothers being on the train, and the singing of Dixie and now, he remembered with a pang of deep hurt, the smile which young John had on his face as he sang about the land of cotton, which was, in fact, not a crop which the valley produced, but was more common in the coastal areas where they planted it year after year, leaching the soil of all its nutrients. Then as the weight of his perfectly formed and untouched body of his brother, John, in his arms, they, he and Immanuel broke from the woods, and first one, then another of John's brothers had looked up, their plates forgotten, dropped and rushing around Uzziah the cries of grief, and Sean sitting there by the fire refusing to look at the body at first.

"Is it him?" he finally asked, not looking up from his plate. He knew who it was, he had heard the cries of his siblings as they walked toward the campfire. He knew.

"Yeah, Pa, it's Johnny," Uzziah had said, and it was

then that the tears had broken from his head and would not stop. He made no sound, but standing there with the barely warm body of his flesh and the flesh of Rahab, Sean took the body and, walking back to the tent where John had slept, he put the boy to bed and covered him up.

The others had looked to Uzziah as if to ask what the hell is Pa doing, but Uzziah just pulled his pipe from his possibles pouch, filled it, sat there by the fire, and lit it up.

He could feel Immanuel's hand on his arm, but with the understanding of many years together, Immanuel did not speak. They both sat there and silently smoked as all Johnny's brothers stood outside the tent where their pa, Sean O'Bannon, had put the boy to bed. No one knew what to do, no one.

Uzziah had gone and talked with General Johnston. They were going to take their dead youngest brother back to the farm in the Shenandoah Valley. "*Of course,*" Johnston had said, "***and since you're already going to be in the valley, join up with Jackson, he would clear it with the Virginia Military Instituted teacher.***" And as soon as they had buried the boy, they were to return to Jackson's camp, but it would be up to them to find it. Jackson was fairly close-mouthed about where he moved his troops and where exactly they would be.

8

Uzziah had built a travois, and John's body, wrapped in the blankets he'd brought from his bed at home, were wrapped around him and tied closed. His head was covered, and the brothers, their pa, and Uzziah's partner, Immanuel, made their way from Manassas back to Strasburg on the Manassas Gap Railroad. They had the coffin, which they bought in Strasburg, put on the stage, which they followed. It looked strange up on the top of the stage, and Uzziah couldn't help but think that poor Johnny would have to be rearranged once he got home. The body was not embalmed, and it would be fairly ripe when they made it home, but what were they to do?

They rented a wagon in Luray and took Johnny the rest of the way home.

When they turned from the Shenandoah main road which followed the river to the farm road which would take them to the house, there was no one in the farmyard, but halfway down the road, all the women were running down the farm road, and looking from face-to-face of those who were riding with the coffin, they made their deductions—Johnny was the missing one, Johnny was dead.

Rahab fell in the road, and Sean had to get off his horse and help her up on the wagon. She made the rest of the journey lying on the coffin and wailing like a banshee.

Whatever had been going on at the farm was stopped. The body was taken to the pump house and washed, and the stink of it wafted toward the house. Rahab, his ma, would have no one with her as she cleaned the body up, and since it was not embalmed, she took the potpourri from all the drawers in the house and stacked them around the body. It had been long enough that the body had lost its rigor, and she dressed the boy in one of Sean's best suits, which she had to alter, but alter it she did. Everyone wanted to help, and even Uzziah had walked out there and looked in.

It was a pitiful sight. John looked bad, but Rahab was carrying on a conversation with him, something about the time he'd left the house at night to see a young girl at another ranch. When she saw Uzziah, she smiled.

"He's real sorry, he done what he done, but we'll make it right," she said as she continued to shorten the pants that would forever be encased in the wooden coffin.

Uzziah walked back to the house, where his sisters and brothers had pretty much been crying since they had brought the body of Johnny home. It was strange to Uzziah that the boy did not want to be called Johnny, he wanted the man's name, John, to be his moniker, and now all anyone ever called him was Johnny. It occurred to him that the Injun way of not repeating the dead person's name again was perhaps better than what was happening at the farmhouse.

It took Rahab two full days with that stinking body to get him the way she wanted him, and when he was brought into the house, all the windows were opened and sashay was spread around, and plenty of wildflowers, but still under it all, there was the smell of his rotting flesh.

They weren't on a time schedule, but they were. If they were to join Jackson's Shenandoah Valley Army, they had to get back north. The papers which were delivered spoke of the victory of the South and the newest famous general of the South, Stonewall Jackson. It occurred to Uzziah and Immanuel both that they had been there when that had happened, and also that Johnny had been there, but lying back in the woods lifeless.

Finally, Rahab agreed that the stinking body should be topped off with the pine top, and they put the coffin on their best wagon, which was the same as the farm wagon, and they followed on foot as Sean drove real slow out to the cemetery. There lay the bodies of stillborn babes which Rahab had hoped to raise up, and some of Sean's people and some of hers. There was plenty of room for more, and Uzziah certainly hoped that the room would not be necessary, and yet, he knew with a family that big, there would be more, maybe even his own carcass would be laid to rest with Johnny, who wanted to be called John.

When they lowered the coffin into the ground, they all expected Rahab to break down completely, but something strange happened. She stood there as Uzziah read scripture, the 23rd Psalm, and something from Philippians, and then a passage about the dead rising on the last day, and when it came time to fill the grave in, Rahab was the first to take the shovel and dump a full load on the top of the coffin. It sounded worse than Uzziah could have ever imagined, but having done that, she turned and, without a tear, walked the distance back to the house and started dinner. That was just the kind of woman she was, and Uzziah realized that he was proud of her for being the stalwart and handsome woman who could take a blow like that, and then cook for her other children.

She never demanded that they did not go back to the war, and she never said anything about revenge, but it was on all their minds, to have their youngest blown senseless, lifeless, it would have been better if his parts had been thrown in different directions, instead, he looked good, except for the smell and the bloating that happened at the end.

When they left the next day, they all had lunches packed and way too much food to take with them, but Rahab insisted, and what were they to do?

She stood on the porch in the front of the house and waved, and waved, even after they had made the main road, and she was but a small dot. They had to keep turning and waving.

Meantime, Hanna had made up her mind. She was busy on the second story of the house. She had commandeered Johnny's clothes and was altering them to fit herself. She would not be the first to take the *pantaloon role* in this war between brothers, and certainly not the last. She was not going to sit home and wait for more brothers to be boxed and brought back. She was going to join and fight, and she didn't care what anyone thought. When she was ready, she would cut off her red hair, and flatten her breasts with bandages, and donning her brother's clothes she would join another unit, some Confederate part where her brothers and her pa did not fight, and by God, she would kill as many of those damned Yankees as she could before this thing ended, and she sincerely hoped she could kill a lot of them.

Of course, she would be missed at home, but for the next few years, her brothers would not know, and by the time they did, she would have established herself, ensconced herself in the Confederate cavalry. She was the best rider of all the children, and Sean had taken extra efforts in helping her to know all about horses. She not only knew how to ride as well as any man, but she also knew remedies and concoctions that could cure a horse if it was going bad.

She felt bad about her ma, Rahab. She knew that she was hurting, having just lost her youngest boy, and she really had no idea what that might feel like, but what good would it do her mother if she stayed there at the farm? She would just be another mourning O'Bannon woman, and she knew herself to be more than simply that.

Her brothers and her pa would be too busy with

their part in the war, which was anything but civil. She would fight and fight, kill and be shot at, and kill some more, and if she made it, she would know that she had not knitted a pillow for her departed brother, Johnny, but stitched bullets into the body of the army which had done him in.

She didn't know exactly what direction she was going to take, she just knew that she couldn't be on the same road as her pa and her surviving brothers. So, she went south toward North Carolina.

Her journey as a man, ironically, was her teaching on what to say and what not to say. She decided early on that reticence was her best friend and that being gregarious would only show her feminine side way too much.

At various points along the road to North Carolina, she met and dealt with all sorts of men, some ruffians, who were anything but kind, and this was her first test as a *young boy*.

She wrote a letter which she mailed to her mother, Rahab O'Bannon. She knew that her mother would be worried about her, but she also knew that if she did not communicate, then she would be thought dead.

Dearest Ma, I have made my way south and am hoping to encounter a cavalry unit to which I will attach myself. I am sorry for leaving with no notice, but the death of our brother John compelled me to take action, so action I took.

When she was nearly at her destination, she stopped at a crossroads store to get provisions.

She brought her horse, a mare named Mandy, to a halt outside the store. There were several men sitting in chairs and spitting tobacco juice over the railing of the porch and onto the dirt. She paid them little attention and went on inside.

While she was inside, those men decided that the good-looking mare the young boy rode was much too fine for such a lad. When he came out, they decided that the mare would be theirs, and to hell with its owner.

"Say, boy, where'd ya steal that there hoss?" the burliest of them spoke.

"My name is *John*," he said, and went on down to where Mandy was tied. She had taken her dead brother's name in honor of his death, and as a reminder of why she was doing what she was doing.

The roughest man who had already spoken to *John* pulled a pistol from his belt and cocked it.

"I say that horse is mine, what do ya say?"

Hanna had always been an excellent shot, and she did have the pistol that Sean had taught her to shoot with her.

She did not hesitate but drew her weapon, and, as it cleared her jacket out of sight of those on the porch, she cocked it, and laying it across the saddle, she fired a shot into the chest of the man who had drawn on her.

The mayhem on the porch was infectious as other men tried to pull iron, and *John,* mounting up, fired into the melee of men who were attempting to steal Mandy. Another man was dropped from his standing position, and shouts and weapons were going off, intended to end the young boy's life.

But she was an experienced horseperson and ran the horse directly away from the porch, presenting only the back side of the horse and her own back as she fired three more times over her shoulder, shattering the store's window and felling another one of the blaggards.

She rode as fast as she could through the woods. Mandy, an excellent jumper, made the necessary jumps over downfalls, and fairly soon, the mayhem at the country store was far behind her.

That night, she cold camped and ate jerky and drank water from a stream. Mandy found plentiful croppings of grass, and the stream was right where she had camped. Once she had calmed down from all the excitement of the gun battle, she began to shake, realizing that she had killed her first man, and that he was not the Yankee whom she had hoped to exact her revenge on. Lying in her blankets, she cried herself to sleep, wondering what she had done, and yet, never, ever thinking about returning to the Shenandoah Valley and her home. She would, by God, find a cavalry unit and become a part of it, if it were the last thing she ever did.

In retrospect, she realized a few days later that that particular encounter had been the best thing that could have happened to her. She had been forged in the heat of battle, and something in her, after killing at least two men and wounding others, something in her turned, and the turning was good. She was John O'Bannon, and she would remain John O'Bannon until she returned home or was shot from the saddle in the middle of a cavalry charge.

By the light of the dying spring sun, she finished her letter to her mother.

I have decided to take my dead brother's name as an omen of good faith. I will find a cavalry unit, join it, and keeping my true identity to myself, I will finish what my youngest brother had not even the first opportunity to begin. I am sorry if this vexes you, or causes you pain, but Mother, there are things that happen to us—She was referring to the early skirmish at the country store—*which turn us from who we had always thought ourselves to be into who we, by God's grace, were always intended to be. Tell Sally, Sarah, and Faith that I love them as always, and that the next time we meet, I will regale them with my stories of being a soldier.*

Your Faithful Servant and in God's Grace I am,
John O'Bannon

Down in southern Virginia, *John O'Bannon* was making her way further and further into the wilderness. She wasn't sure where she was now, and she began to have the feeling that she might just be lost. How was she to find a cavalry unit and join up? What if she just kept wandering around?

"Hold it right there!" a male voice commanded. She reached under her coat for her slide revolver that her oldest brother had given her.

"Ifn ya bring that out, I will shoot ya outta the saddle, young man," the melodious voice commanded.

She pulled her hand back and turned in the saddle toward the voice. To her surprise, it was a Confederate cavalryman. He was tall in the saddle and had sandy hair and the nicest beard on his face that she had ever seen. His blue eyes pierced directly into her heart, and the phrase *love at first sight* popped into her head. How ridiculous, he was holding a Griswold pistol on her, and his finger was tightening on the trigger. Still, the handsome cavalryman's uniform fit him perfectly, and the smile that was creeping across his lips said a whole lot.

"Yer just a boy," he said and uncocked the piece. "What are ya doin' out here wandering around, are ya lost?" he asked as he put the Griswold away. "Sorry, I'm Sergeant Stark Simmons, what be yer name?"

She had the strongest desire to tell him her name was Hanna Jane O'Bannon, but instead her voice said, "John O'Bannon, sir."

"Ya don't have to call me *sir,* I work for a living. So, what are ya doin' out here?" he asked in his deep and pleasant Virginia accent.

She loved his voice, his mannerism, his face, the way he sat his horse, it was almost as good as hers.

"O'Bannon, cat got yer tongue?" he asked.

"No, sir, sorry, sir, I mean. I'm lost, I'm looking for a cavalry unit to join, I wanna kill some Yankees," she said. She didn't have to disguise her voice, all her brothers had been jealous of her so-called whiskey voice, she had spoken that way since she was a child.

Stark chuckled and not to himself. "Well, what makes ya think a whelp of a boy, still wet behind the ears, has what it takes to be a Confederate cavalryman?"

The question was unanswered because several shots whizzed by both their ears, and then the reports. Hanna looked back, and it was what was left of the porch crew, they must have followed her. Without thinking, she and Stark kicked their horses into high gear. And she could see that she had reacted faster than the sergeant and was blazing a trail through the deadfall. There was an open field to the right, but she stayed in the deadfall and woods and drove her horse Mandy deeper into that troubled area.

"What are ya doin'!?!" Stark asked, but she kept at it with him on her and Mandy's heels.

They heard a horse cry out behind them and a shout from one of the three men who were following. When Stark looked about, one of the pursuers' horses had gone down and fallen on its rider; the other two were having trouble with the deadfall.

Finally, the woods gave out, and a large field opened up in front of them. Hanna kicked Mandy into high gear, and she galloped out like nobody's business. He rode up alongside her and shouted, "Where'd ya learn to ride like this?"

Instead of answering Stark, she looked behind her and shouted back, "Go left. I'll go right!" and then she reined Mandy hard right and Stark his horse hard left just as bullets occupied the spaces that they had vacated.

One of the men had dismounted and had out his long gun and was cracking away at them. When he saw their defensive maneuvers, he mounted back up and rode hard to catch up with his partner, who had taken the left route toward Stark. He would follow the boy from the store and even the score.

Hanna pulled Mandy to a sliding stop, yanked her Winchester from the saddle boot, and aimed at the rider coming her way. She fired, and the man's horse stumbled and they both went down.

Sergeant Stark was looking over toward where *John O'Bannon* was aiming at the man who was close behind him. Another crack from O'Bannon's rifle and the man chasing Stark threw his hands up and tumbled off the back of his still running horse.

They met in the middle of the field, and Stark was shaking his head.

"I apologize, John. Haven't seen shooting like that, not to mention the fine job of yer navigating yer horse through the deadfall, in years."

"Mandy knows what to do, I just give her her head," Hanna said.

"And the shooting, where in God's name did ya learn that?" Stark asked.

"My pa, Sean O'Bannon, he's a crack shot, and of all the sons he has, I'm the closest to his marksmanship," Hanna said.

Stark rode up close to her horse, and tail to head, he offered his hand in friendship. They shook, and Stark spoke. "Jeb's not far from here, ifn ya still want to ride with us, I'd say what just happened is an open invitation."

They shook hands, and Hanna's heart went out to the sergeant. She was smitten. Of all the horse trading, backstabbing, dry gulching things to happen to her. Here she was, finally about to get to kill some people who were actually Yankees, and her heart was playing tricks with her. Well, she didn't care how she felt about the handsome, rogue of that young sergeant, she wasn't going to let those batting beautiful blues enhance her, or the way his uniform snugged to the muscular frame of his body, nor the way his skintight pant legs were thrust into his knee-high cavalry boots have a thing to do with what was about to happen.

Hanna insisted they check on the horse that had

stumbled for no other reason to make sure the man riding it was dead. They approached the fallen horse stealthily, and when they got there, the man was shot dead, but the horse had stepped into a gopher hole, and its leg was broken.

Hanna dismounted and soothed the horse by whispering to it and stroking its head. The animal calmed down, and as quick as a wink, she drew her harmonica pistol and fired a shot between its eyes.

Stark jerked in the saddle. He knew the horse had to be put down, but the way John was speaking to the horse had captivated him. The sudden pull of the weapon and the putting down without hesitation gave Stark a new respect for the young man.

Stark Simmons was an only child, but only because his younger brother had drowned when the boy was twelve. Stark had been with his brother out at the lake, and his attention had been distracted by a sweet young thing that he thought he might be interested in, and when he turned back to the lake, his brother was nowhere to be seen.

He'd dove and dove until he did find Rudy's body. He was hanging halfway to the bottom with his arms out like he'd given up. His ma and pa were not happy that he'd let the boy drown, and there was a sense in which they had never forgiven him. Well, at least that's the way he felt about it. This John O'Bannon was in some ways the spitting image of his younger brother, even though over the years his memory of the boy had slipped a bit. He carried with him a small daguerreotype of his brother that had been taken the spring before he drowned. It was in his tent, he would have to look once again to see just how close the resemblance was between John and Rudy.

They rode together talking about this or that, and Hanna was enthralled, but refused to give in. How could she kill Yankees if he knew she was a girl? It was simple; she couldn't. If her identity were known, she would be sent home, and that would be that. So far, she had killed four Virginians who, indeed, might have been scum, but they were not Yankees. She was supposed to be taking a toll on those who had killed her youngest brother, not other Virginians, no matter how despicable they were!

The ride to Jed Stuart's camp wasn't that long, but it was circuitous. When they rode in, Stark took them immediately to General Stuart's tent.

"Stay mounted and stay alert, and by the way, sit straighter in the saddle," the sergeant admonished.

Hanna looked about at the milling of the cavalrymen, some cooking, some sewing, some reading, some just sitting around smoking. They looked at her but paid her no more mind than they did anything else. This reinforced the opinion that Hanna had made of the male species. She had always thought that having a penis wasn't any reason for society to think that men were somehow superior. Sure, they were generally stronger physically, and built taller and with greater stamina, but a lot of women, herself included, had stamina enough, and giving birth wasn't exactly a sport that was to be engaged in indifferently.

When she looked back at the general's tent, the sergeant was holding the tent flap open, and the general was staring out at her. His piercing eyes seemed to know that she was a woman, but then the sergeant let the tent flap go, and in a few moments, he was out, mounting back up.

"Well?" she asked, half expecting him to escort her back home.

"You're now a part of General Jeb Stuart's First Virginia Cavalry, congratulations!" Stark said and extended his hand, and they shook. A spark traveled from their naked bare hands to her heart, and she did all she could to keep from wanting to kiss the sergeant there and then.

"There's only one stipulation. How old did ya say ya were?"

"Sixteen," she said.

"And yer parents know yer here?"

"Yes, of course, my pa is fighting, too," she said.

"With whom?"

"General Jackson," she said.

"Well, he's up in Winchester, not likely y'all run into him, sorry," Stark said.

Sorry, she thought, she was thrilled. The further away her brothers and her pa were from her, the better this would work out.

"Well, there is a stipulation, John," the sergeant said.

"Oh?" she asked.

"Until ya become familiar with all aspects of the Cavalryman's code and all the maneuvers, yer to bunk with me, and we ride as close as we can, understand?"

The expression on Hanna's face might have given her away if anyone knew that she was anything but a young boy. She hesitated because what Stark had just said was the answer to her prayers. She was fighting it, she really was, but sleeping in the same tent, riding with him at all times, what the hell was she going to do!?!

"John? Do ya accept the terms?"

"Yes, fine, whatever ya say," she said, and unfortunately, that was exactly what she meant.

The first night that *John O'Bannon* spent in Sergeant Stark's tent, he went to sleep rather quickly. It seemed that everything she had wanted was coming true. She had found a cavalry unit, not only a cavalry unit, but the best one. Hanna had heard about Jed Stuart, and she knew that being with General Stuart, she would be in a position to kill Yankees all day long. He was known for his daring-do, and he did not avoid a skirmish, not for anything.

Hanna fell asleep that night, saying her prayers to Father and thanking him for putting her in a position to do as much harm to the Federals as she could. Before this war ended, she would enact the revenge she had in mind. True, John O'Bannon died at the age of sixteen years, but the resurrected Johnny was in a position to take out the enemy of his family and put right the scales upon which his body had been sacrificed.

Sergeant Stark did not go to sleep at all, at first. When he heard the heavy breathing of the—well, they were going to give him the rank of private in the Confederate cavalry, Gen. Stuart had decided—and when Stark knew that the private was asleep, he rummaged through his bags and found the daguerreotype and taking it closer to the cot on which the private slept he held a candle over John O'Bannon's face, and holding the picture close to the private's face, he sucked in a breath. They did look alike.

It was almost as if God was giving the sergeant another chance to take care of his brother, and who knew, maybe this time, he could do it right.

"What's goin' on?" John had awakened and asked Stark.

"Uh, uh," Stark said as he stumbled back away from the cot, "nothin' it's just yer a dead ringer fer someone I once knew," Sergeant Stark announced in the dark, the candle having gone out.

"Oh," was all Hanna could say as she lay there.

Stark got back in his bunk and said a hasty *good-night* and rolled away from Hanna.

What the heck was he doing? Did he suspect that he was a she? Did she resemble some long-lost friend? When she'd awakened and looked at the sergeant, he hadn't seen her looking at him at first, and really, all she wanted to do was to draw him close to her, and kiss that flat line of a mouth which he hid so successfully beneath that mustache, and pull him onto the cot, but then what did she know?

She decided that she would never mention what had happened that night. Better to leave it alone, better to have them both think that it was a dream, a night thing which was not spoken of in the day.

The next morning, Hanna was up later than the sergeant, and when she pulled back the flap on the tent, he was sitting next to the fire. Coffee smell surrounded the campsite, and grits were bubbling in a pot, and bacon was frying in a pan. Hanna was hungry, and she had the opportunity to look at the man whom she may indeed be falling in love with, but when he turned, his demeanor was different.

"Don't just stand there, Private, do yer latrine duty and gather more wood fer the fire!" he growled at her.

She was thankful that the Victorian morals were in place, and that even men did not do their business with other men, but all slipped off to do the necessaries. As she squatted behind some bushes far from the camp, she relieved herself and wondered what she had gotten herself into.

9

The O'Bannon brothers, plus their pa Sean and Uzziah's mountain man partner of many years, had made it back to what was now being called the Shenandoah Army of the Confederacy, with Thomas Jonathan *Stonewall* Jackson in charge. Soon after they arrived in Winchester, Jackson summoned all his scouts to a meeting.

Jackson had taken a modest home within the city of Winchester, and his wife had come up from Lexington to be with him. When the six scouts arrived, Jackson met them at the front door.

"Gentlemen, gentlemen, come in, come in," he cordially welcomed them to his temporary home.

They walked in, and Mrs. Jackson, Mary Anne, was gathering up her knitting from the table she was seated next to.

"Who are these gentlemen, Jonathan?"

"They're my scouts, my eyes and ears for the coming campaign, darling," he said, and that was sufficient for her as she retired to the back of the home.

"She's lovely," Immanuel commented, and Jackson gave him the eye, then he softened.

"Yes, yes, Mary Anne is lovely. This war, as you can imagine, has not exactly been a boon to anyone's marriage," he said, then led them into a large kitchen where a large table had cups all around.

"There is coffee on the stove, and if you'll forgive me, I cannot partake of it late at night, it upsets my stomach, but please help yourselves," Jackson said.

The men gathered around the stove and the cups were filled right there, they all took it black.

"There was supposed to be seven of you. Does anyone know where the Indian is?" Jackson asked.

"Didn't know there was an Injun scout?" one of the older men said, then added, "Thought they was all scoutin' fer the North," one of the men said, as Uzziah and Immanuel looked at each other. *No*, they both thought, *that would be too good to be true*."

Just then, there came a knock at the door.

"'Cuse me," Jackson said, and went and opened it, then shouted, "Here he is!"

When the six men turned, it was as if it were a dream. How could he have known where to scout and whom to scout for?

Abooksigun walked in, and he looked just as he did the last time they had seen him. He seemed to be one of those individuals who just looked the same, no matter what. His traditional leggings had moccasins at the end, and he had a belt of shell-decorated sheepskin turned so the woolly part was showing at the top and bottom. But instead of the traditional deerskin shirt, he wore a cloth shirt with a buckskin jacket over it. There were a couple of eagle feathers in his long hair, and they hung down his back.

Abooksigun grunted happily as the two mountain men made their way into the living room. Uzziah grabbed him up first, and their hug was warm and long, then Immanuel took Uzziah's place. None of them had said anything, so Jackson spoke up.

"Well, this is a good thing, ya'll know each other then?" Jackson asked.

"Yes, General," Immanuel said, "ya could say that." The three men laughed.

"This is good, this is very good. You three will be assigned similar scouting jobs, and in that way, we can increase the area of reconnaissance. Since we will have no cavalry in the valley, I intend to make my soldiers the cavalry," Jackson said and looked to the six scouts for their reactions.

"Hey," one of the other scouts said, "I don't git it, either they're foot soldiers, or they ride horses, right?"

"Can anyone guess what I'm talking 'bout?" Jackson asked, grinning mischievously.

"Men will be horses," Abooksigun said in his deep voice.

Jackson laughed like a hyena, and the other three scouts looked at Jackson as if he'd lost his mind.

"You know yer friend, don't ya, mountain man," Jackson said, looking at Immanuel. "Tell us all what he means?" Jackson asked.

"Ifn yer a foot soldier in Jackson's Valley Army ya'll be traveling as fast as a horse, or ya won't be travelin' at all!" Immanuel said.

Jackson just pointed to Immanuel and said, "Then

can ya guess what yer jobs will be when yer not scouting?"

Everyone looked at Immanuel, but it was Uzziah who answered, "We'll be the bear chasing the men."

"God love ya fer yer sense, man," Jackson said. "Ya'll will be riding herd on my cavalry, seeing that they keep up!"

"And ifn they don't," one of the other scouts asked.

"Well, let's just say that duty to me is next to God, and a man who shirks it has disappointed God Himself," Jackson said.

There was a grumbling among the scouts as if they regarded duty in the same manner.

"Now, on a more pleasant note I'd like ya all to meet my wife, Mary Anne, since ya'll all weren't here when she left the room," Jackson said and he went back into the farthest reaches of the house, and they could all hear them talking, but couldn't make out exactly what they said, then Jackson returned a bit red-faced.

He looked up at the scouts and said, "I can command an army under fire with grape shot and Minie balls whizzing about, but I can't command my wife. What does that say 'bout me?" They weren't sure if he was really asking or if it was just a statement.

"It says yer a smarter man, General Jackson, than any of us gave ya credit fer," Immanuel said, and everyone laughed as the general showed them to the door.

John O'Bannon, alias Hanna O'Bannon, wintered right there in southern Virginia and northern North

Carolina, just south of Richmond, with General J.E.B. Stuart's cavalry, which she now knew to be the 1st Virginia Cavalry of the Cavalry Corps of the Army of Northern Virginia. She couldn't have been prouder. She was going to make a name for her dead brother that would live on long after him, and his name, not hers, would be recorded in the annals of the 1st Virginia Cavalry.

Sometimes in winter camp, she wondered how these men, these boys she joshed with, she ate with, she drilled with, did not have an inkling that she was a woman. She kept her breasts bound tightly, and her new 1st Virginia Cavalry uniform was loose-fitting, and she guessed that they just thought her a boy, who was slender, and could fight and ride like hell.

And winter camp for the 1st Virginian wasn't a rest. General Stuart was known for his discipline and the way he trained and retrained his men and horses. There would be no surprises that these cavalrymen were not ready for. They trained fording rivers, again and again, in shallow and deep waters. They trained charging with sabers drawn, and then they trained retreating, and both of these over and over again. Hanna began to recognize the different bugle calls that indicated each maneuver, it became a second language to her, and she guessed that that was the reason they trained as much as they did.

Then, there were the nights when she slept not four feet from the man, Sergeant Stark, and she heard him mumble in his dreams, and sometimes call out a name, it must have been his dead younger brother, that she realized she favored ever so slightly.

She would lie awake on some nights aching to be in

his arms, to have him hold her more than the brotherly hugs, or his beefy arm around her shoulder. Of course, if she were to do what she wanted to do, the masquerade of being her younger brother would come to an end, and this must never happen. She forced down the feelings of—what was it?—she could only imagine that it was love for this man whom she was under as a protégé, a man that she both admired and wondered at his lack of seeing. All she had done was cut her hair like a boy, and don boy's clothes. Was the difference in the sexes that simple? Strange to be falling for someone who imagined you to be the opposite of what you were, very strange.

From his winter camp in Winchester, Jackson had determined that his Army of the Shenandoah would attack Dam #5 on the Potomac, which would interrupt and hopefully dry up the C & O Canal and stop coal shipments to Washington and make it uncomfortable for the Union.

He took an expeditionary force and over a period of days between the 7th of December 1861 to the 20th, the intrepid Confederate soldiers, mostly Irish, climbed into the icy waters of the Potomac and wacked away with shovels and other tools at the dam. They were sniped on at times, and then artillery was brought in, and for a while, Jackson's artillery drove the Federals back, but then Federal artillery was brought up, and the cliffs on the heights where Jackson's artillery had the advantage of firing down on the enemy were exposed to a withering fire and had to retreat.

Snipers on both sides were put in various pump houses and sniped at their enemy. Immanuel and Uzziah were a part of that, but finally, both pump houses were destroyed by the opposing sides' cannons, and the men had to desert their positions like rats from a sinking ship.

Immanuel and Uzziah quickly melted into the woods, avoiding being sniped as they retreated. Finally, in the third week of December, Jackson himself went down to the Potomac and passed out tools, and the whiskey rations were increased so that even Immanuel got into the chilly waters and tried as best he could to make a dent in Dam #5, but all they managed to do was make the dam weaker.

The Federals charged that no damage was done, and Jackson's report made it seem like they had done some damage. All in all, few men were actually lost in what could only be considered a non-battle with interesting sniping going on.

Back in Winchester, Uzziah and Immanuel were simply glad to be where no one was trying to shoot them. It reminded them so much of the incident at the O'Bannon farm when a sniper had pinned them and Abooksigun down, until they left that particular sniper hanging dead from the tree across the valley. All three men agreed that two such incidents were enough for a lifetime.

"What the hell were ya thinkin' getting into that cold damned water?" Uzziah castigated Immanuel.

"Well, hell, it seemed to me that those Irish, and I might add, you're one of 'em, weren't doin' shite on that dam. I mean, how hard could it be, chop a damned hole in it, and be done," Immanuel said, his shoulders still shaking from being in the nearly freezing water.

"I'll tell ya what I know, there was only one reason ya got down in that freezing stream," Uzziah said, taking the moral high ground.

"And don't start in on the whiskey thing," Immanuel interrupted him.

"Why not? If Jackson hadn't tripled the rations on the whiskey, ya never would have risked yer health on something so stupid. Hell, ifn Frederick and Max had been there, they coulda blown that silly dam to smithereens!" Uzziah was getting on his high horse now.

"Hey, Abooksigun," Immanuel said, "ya got any hooch?"

"Injun and whiskey not good friends," Abooksigun said as he was curled up in the corner of the tent the three men shared.

"Don't give that Injun bullshite, ya got any or not?" Immanuel came back.

"Maybe."

"Well, maybe send that there bottle over this way," Immanuel said, still shaking. "I gots to warm this chere carcass up."

Uzziah grabbed the bottle as it was being passed, "Whiskey don't do nothin' but lower yer body temperature, it only makes ya feel warmer when in fact, yer not!"

"Save the natural history lecture," Immanuel said as he grabbed the bottle, and the two men looked like they would do more harm than what whiskey had done.

Abooksigun grabbed the bottle, "What the hell ya two arguing fer? Ifn he want whiskey, give whiskey," he said and handed the bottle to Immanuel. "Two old squaws bickering over nothin' that's what ya are!"

"Thank ye," Immanuel said as he tipped the bottle and drank.

"Why do I like white men. I often ask," Abooksigun said.

"Got ya an answer yet?" Uzziah asked.

"Almost," Abooksigun said as he got the bottle, drank, and passed it to Uzziah, who tilted it skyward.

"Easy! Easy!" Immanuel nearly shouted.

"Old squaws, that's what ya are! Just old squaws!" Abooksigun said with disgust.

10

As spring burgeoned in Virginia, and the bare trees gave way to buds, and birds making nests, it seemed to Hanna as if there must be something to do besides train, train, train. It was just after the first week in June that a cadre of officers and a couple of generals rode into General Stuart's camp and the flamboyant General Stuart, who, when not training, wore a red sash and had a cape with a red lining, and a cavalryman's hat with a ostrich plume in it, was as surprised as everyone else when the news circled the camp that the newly appointed commander of the Army of Northern Virginia, General Robert Edward Lee was the main visitor who had come to see General Stuart.

The camp was as quiet as a morgue while the two generals held a closed-flap meeting in General Stuart's command tent, the same one Hanna had sat outside on her horse, Mandy, when she first arrived.

"What do ya think they're talking 'bout?" Hanna

asked Sergeant Simmons, who had a cup of coffee in his hand, but wasn't drinking it.

"Well, my good friend John, that would be the question of the hour, now, wouldn't it?" Stark said as he sipped the cold brew, then spit it out, throwing the rest of the cup in the fire where it sizzled nicely.

The day was a perfect spring day in Virginia, and Hanna couldn't help but think about what her ma and sisters might be up to. It was time to plant, and since it was a farm, that's exactly what they would be doing. No word that the Yankees had managed to get down into the Shenandoah since Jackson and his *cavalry* were blocking the way. It was a strange nomenclature for foot soldiers, but it was said they wore it proudly. The only ones on horses were the officers and scouts. It was the alacrity with which Jackson was able to move those on foot that had brought about the name, and she wondered how her pa and brothers were liking marching all over northern Virginia.

"You're lost in thought," Stark noted as he gave John one of his wry smiles. He had at least fifteen different ways of smiling, and Hanna had memorized all of them. This one said he wanted to be talked to, to pass the time, and nothing more. He really didn't care about her thoughts or the thoughts of John O'Bannon, he was simply bored with waiting on finding out what Generals Lee and Stuart had up their sleeves. Stark had told her, 'This was a war of secrets, and it was best to keep yours,' in more ways than one, she imagined.

"Just thinking of home and all the work my ma and sisters have to carry."

"Ya wanna go help, don't ya?" he asked.

"Yes, I do, but I know where my duty lies, and if we are unsuccessful in our endeavors, then all will be lost."

"Who taught ya to talk like that?" Stark asked.

"My ma and pa may not have been formally educated, but the Bible and Shakespeare are the most used books in our home."

"Shakespeare, really?"

"On cold winter nights after dessert, when all the chores and feeding was done, we'd open the big book, and take different parts. You haven't experienced the Bard without doing that," she said, wistfully remembering.

"Well, when this war is won, I'd like to meet yer ma, and sisters, say, are any of them good-looking?"

Now that was going too far, but what could Hanna say? Well, she could tell the truth.

"Yes, you'd probably fall in love with them all," Hanna said.

"It'll be a while before the generals are through. Tell me about them," Stark said as he sat back and for the first time since General Lee arrived, seemed to relax.

"Well, Sally is the oldest—"

"A spinster?!?"

"Are ya gonna let me tell you, or not?"

"Sorry, go ahead," Stark said as he closed his eyes, perhaps better to imagine what Hanna would describe.

"Sally is the oldest. Her hair is long and golden, and I don't mean that dishwater blond that some women call blond, I mean, when the sun hits it, it shines so that you nearly have to look away. She's a fine figure of a woman, even though she had a daughter—"

"She's married!"

"Stark, stop it, let me tell the tale," Hanna said.

"Fine," he said, resigned to just listening.

"She was married, but her daughter—I will not say her name, it's too painful," Hanna said, remembering Uzziah telling the family the Injun practice of never repeating the names of those who had passed. "Anyway, her husband took to the bottle after the death of their daughter, and she left him in Harper's Ferry and moved back in with the family. She has a nip now and then, and I'll bet ya like that in a woman," Hanna said, and Stark opened his eyes and looked at John O'Bannon, wondering how he knew such a thing. "Anyway, she's looking for a good man, and who knows?"

"How about the other sisters, ya have three right?" Stark asked.

"Yeah, three, but the others are probably too young to wed," Hanna said to see if he would jump at the bait, which he did.

"How old?"

"Sarah's twenty-one and Faith is twenty—"

"God, that's not young!"

"Well, it certainly ain't old," Hanna said, thinking of her own age, which she had lied about. She was eighteen, pretending to be sixteen. She wondered what he would think of her age.

"Describe the last two to me," Stark asked, but just then, the two generals who had been, as it were, behind closed doors emerged from General Stuart's command tent, and it was as if a stone had been thrown into a still pond. From those just outside the command tent, the motion of men moving and talking moved out like the ripples in the water.

"They're through," Stark said as he stood, perhaps

imagining that he might be introduced to General Lee, but those hopes were dashed when General Lee mounted up on Traveler—everyone knew the name of Lee's gray horse—and the party which had so unexpectedly come in just as unexpectantly rode out.

Hanna looked at Sergeant Stark, his body all tense as a drawn wire, and this was one of her favorite ways he could be. He was ready for anything, everything, and she loved him, did she think that (?) for being so eager, and wondered if that tenseness, that eagerness would be in the marital bed, and she forbade herself to think further.

General Jeb Stuart made a circular motion with his gloved hand, and that was the same motion made for rounding up when they were on horseback, and all those in command, from officers to sergeants, literally ran toward where he was standing. Those men would be briefed on what was happening, at least as much as Stuart was given to let them know, and then, hopefully, they would mount up and go kill some Yankees!

Mt. Jackson, Virginia

Stonewall in the spring of 1862 called a meeting with all commanders and scouts. They all thought they might get information on Stonewall's plans for the coming campaign, but as usual, they were sorely disappointed.

Jackson entered the meeting tent, and everyone there got silent.

"Gentlemen, thank you for comin'. I have some important news which will not instill confidence, but hopefully will instill a sense of urgency in what this Army of the Shenandoah will accomplish within the next few months."

Someone raised a hand, which Jackson waved off.

"No questions until ya know what we're up against and what we are about to accomplish by the grace of God, and his Almighty will. An army of some 100,000 men under General George B. McClellan is threatening Richmond, the capital of our beloved Confederacy, from the southeast." There were groans around the room.

"Please save your feelings until ya know exactly what we're up against. If McLellan's men were not enough, General Irwin McDowell, with 30,000 men near Fredericksburg, will advance on Richmond from the north.

"Having spoken with General Lee, and in conjunction with his advice to President Jefferson Davis, we, the men of the Shenandoah Army of the Confederacy, will create within the valley such a nuisance that the Federals will be paralyzed with fear and draw troops away from both those armies' facing advancement on Richmond."

Colonel Turner Ashby raised his hand.

"Yes, Colonel Ashby, what is it?"

"Then, you do have a plan by which we will upset and unsettle these Federal troops?"

"Yes, of course, I do," Jackson replied.

"Could you inform us of those plans so that all the commanders might be on the same page?" Ashby asked.

"Yes, I could," Jackson said, and he paused, and

everyone seemed relieved that they would soon know Jackson's plans, "but I won't."

There was a collective groan from the commanders who were growing tired of Jackson's closed-mouth attitudes about orders. Some commanders just wanted to know where they were going next so that they might point their supply trains in the right direction the night before.

"An army," Jackson continued, "is only as safe and as good as the secrets which its general is able to keep. I do know what we will do, and when we will do it, but you other commanders must wait until the hour is ripe to receive yer orders. No, written messages or gossiped information is going to sink this army's efforts to battle the Federals, is that understood?"

It was understood all right, but they didn't like it one bit, some commanders, some generals complained as far up as the President of the Confederacy itself, but Jackson was by now famous for keeping his own council, and since he had been the hero of 1st Manassas, he stood in the enviable position of being the Confederacy's only hero besides Beauregard who had bombed Ft. Sumter and made the Union surrender at Charleston harbor.

"We will have a vigorous campaign, I can tell you that, and even what I know as I gain intelligence from Ashby's cavalry, even what I know will change, for an army is only as good as its immediate reactions to the situations at hand. Dismissed," Jackson said, and before he left the tent, he signaled to three of his scouts who were standing nearby. "Come with me," he said.

Outside the command tent, Uzziah, Immanuel, and Abooksigun followed Jackson down a few rows of tents.

The night sky was filled with the panoply of stars. The Milky Way seemed to be giving enough light to follow the general to his private tent on Mt. Jackson. He went in, leaving the tent flap open. All three scouts followed him as Jackson took a seat behind his field desk.

"You three will accompany Colonel Ashby's Cavalry to Winchester, where I hope he will engage elements of Union General Shields' division. As soon as Ashby has any intelligence on the strength and movement of the Union armies in that area, you are to return here, and bring that intelligence to me, and for my ears only, do the three of ya understand yer orders?"

"Yes, General," Uzziah said, and the other two nodded their heads.

"Then, get some rest, you will leave with Colonel Ashby at 0500 hours, and you will not discuss this with anyone, understood?"

"Yes, General," this time it was Immanuel who answered.

"You, your name's Abooksigun, I understand," Jackson said.

Abooksigun nodded his head in agreement.

"I just wish all my men had your reticence in speaking. It seems to me that my words are not wasted on you, and that they would never be repeated, and I just want to thank you fer that," Jackson said.

"Welcome," Abooksigun said, and the three of them exited the tent.

They walked back to the tent that the three of them shared, and nothing was spoken until they were out of the chill of the air and inside.

"Old Blue Lights likes ya, Injun," Immanuel teased.

"Not me, but lack of gossip," Abooksigun said.

"Yeah, we both know someone who can't stop talking once he's had a nip or two," Uzziah teased.

"Yer no better—"

"In my cups, I'm not, but the frequency of that is nothin' compared to ya," Uzziah said.

"Oh, temperance is yer middle name, ain't it, yer nothin' but a jack Mormon!?!"

"Ladies," Abooksigun said. "Not tonight, early we ride."

The two mountain men looked at each other as if they could have continued arguing for hours, and they probably could have, but Immanuel thought, the Injun was right, riding out early with Ashby, he would need his rest. He hated to admit it, but he wasn't as young as he used to be.

As Ashby's Cavalry rode toward Winchester and engaged elements of Union General James Shields' division on the southern outskirts of Winchester, Jackson's small army of 3,500 men marched north from Mt. Jackson.

The skirmish outside Winchester and the intelligence gathered from the people of Winchester led Ashby to believe that the Federals were withdrawing from the valley.

Abooksigun, Uzziah, and Immanuel rode up fast to Jackson's foot soldiers and found the general walking his horse, Fancy, behind the last of his men, which would essentially be considered *drag* if it were a cattle drive.

"General Jackson," Uzziah said as he rode up.

"You're surprised to find me trailing my men, aren't ya?"

"Well, yeah, a bit," Immanuel admitted as he, Uzziah, and Abooksigun got off their horses and walked with Jackson.

"Have ya news from Ashby?"

"We do, sir. It seems most of the Federals have withdrawn from Winchester, and this is confirmed by some of the town's own people," Uzziah told Jackson.

"Good, good, very good, then we shall attack the Federals at Kernstown," Jackson said, and mounting up and kicking Fancy, his horse up into a trot as he rode along the side of the trail to the front of his troops.

"Kernstown is the other direction," Immanuel protested.

"Yeah, well, anybody watchin' will never suspect, will they?" Uzziah added.

Kernstown and Winchester were so close that they might have been considered the same town. Jackson's intelligence suggested that going to Winchester through Kernstown seemed to be the best way to attack the Federals.

Halfway into Kernstown, it became evident that the information which Ashby's Cavalry had gathered was inaccurate, to say the least. The Federals resisted the Confederate advance and pushed back. Jackson, thinking it was just stiff resistance before they retreated, pushed his men forward until it looked like they could push no more. It was then that Jackson, the two mountain men, and Abooksigun rode up on a little knoll and surveyed the battlefield.

What they saw was not encouraging. The Federals had more reinforcements come from just about every direction, and it looked very much like the band of some 3,500 Confederates was about to be engulfed.

"This looks bad, very bad," Jackson mumbled almost to himself, then he raised his arms, bowed his head, and began to pray.

"General, sorry to interrupt, but I got a way outta this," Immanuel said.

General Jackson stopped praying, lowered his arms, and stared at Immanuel.

"I know, sir, I interrupted your talk with God, but this reminds me of an old grizzly bear I once saw. She had cubs, and me and few others had surrounded her, well, when it looked like we could take her and her cubs, cub meat is so sweet, she went berserk."

"What do ya mean?" the general asked.

"Well, in spite of the fact that we were drillin' holes in her, she got up, roared, and advanced on all of us. Uzziah, ya remember?"

"It's true, General Jackson, she was swiping the air and chargin' us all, and I'll never forget that growl!"

"What happened then?" Jackson asked.

"We pulled out and left her and her cubs be," Immanuel said.

"Same with porcupine," Abooksigun said.

"Porcupine?" Jackson asked.

"When cornered, they spray their quills everywhere, and while their predator is full of quills, they retreat."

"I see," Jackson mused.

"But must yell, battle cry will scare," Abooksigun added.

Jackson rode down from the promontory and went to his officers who were gathered down below him. He spoke for only a moment, looked at his pocket chronometer, and pointed at it with purpose, then rode back up to where the two mountain men and Abooksigun sat their horses, while the officers rode off to their commands.

"Let's hope that you all are right," Jackson mumbled, then he pulled out his pocket watch and looked at it gravely.

Not more than ten minutes had passed before a terrible cry went up from the Confederate lines. It made all their blood run cold, even Jackson, and he had been expecting it.

Then the most amazing thing happened. The beleaguered rebels charged straight out and into the lines of the Federals, who were so caught off guard, either by the harrowing screams of the Confederates, which persisted as they charged, or perhaps it was the manner and ferocity with which the band of less than 4,000 was widening the circle and pushing the Federals back.

"I have told my commanders that once we had them on the run, they were to leave a small portion of men while the rest retreated," Jackson said. And it was then that the yelling stopped, and the majority of men pulled back, leaving a small band to place withering fire on the Federals.

"I shall call this the *mother bear porcupine defense,*

thank ye, thank ye, gentlemen. This just may have worked," Jackson said as he lost no time urging Fancy down the hill and toward his retreating army.

THE WAR OFFICE, WASHINGTON

President Lincoln stood tall and gaunt among many generals who were so much shorter than he was, it looked as if he may be from another world altogether. As they looked down on a map with toy soldiers on it, placed wherever Federal troops were assigned, a courier came in. He was out of breath and beleaguered, having just come from the battlefield at Kernstown.

He spoke to an adjutant, who listened, then spoke.

"Mr. President, you may want to hear what this man has to say."

Lincoln turned his unnaturally large and gaunt head toward the adjutant and the courier, then with one large hand, encouraged the man to come forward. Both adjutant and courier walked briskly over.

"What is it, young man?" Lincoln asked.

"The rebels, Mr. President, the rebels at Kernstown," the man had to stop, he was out of breath.

"What about them, son?" Lincoln asked.

"They are numerous and fighting as if it were literally the end of times," the courier said.

"Then our intelligence must be wrong," Lincoln said to himself.

"And that's not all, they screamed as they ran forward into our musket fire!"

"Screamed—as in pain?" Lincoln asked.

"No, sir, as if possessed by the Devil himself," the courier added.

Lincoln looked back at the map and, picking up a hook that lay along the map, moved many soldiers from McClennan's army, and even more from General Irwin McDowell's troops who had gathered at Frederiksberg. He moved all those troops to the valley of the Shenandoah.

The generals gathered around the table, looking at Lincoln dubiously.

"It seems Stonewall Jackson has fooled us again, gentlemen. There are many more troops in the Shenandoah than we were informed. We must move many from the 30,000 of McDowell's army near Fredericksburg and even more from McClellan's 100,000 troops southeast of Richmond."

Wire operators who were stationed in the war room got their instructions from their various generals and they were jerking lightning, sending out messages to both the Federal commanders.

Once the feign of an extreme attack and the screaming of the banshees had scared the bejesus out of the Federals, Stonewall's brigade withdrew safely enough.

Far enough away for safety, they set up camp, such as it was again. Abooksigun, Uzziah, and Immanuel camped away from the troops as was the custom of all the scouts, some of them simply didn't stay in the camp, but showed up the next morning, staying God knew where.

Uzziah had put together a meager meal of biscuits,

beans, and bacon, their staple. They ate in silence, and Uzziah knew that something was on Immanuel's mind. Once supper tin plates and pans were put away, all three men took to looking after their weapons. The night was cool, but not cold, really a perfect night for sleeping in the open as the two mountain men and their friend Abooksigun had done for most of their lives.

"Just spit it out," Uzziah said in a normal voice.

Abooksigun looked at Uzziah and pulled his legs up under him as if he were getting ready for another one of their arguments.

Immanuel looked at his partner with a pained expression, then began.

"Look, sometimes a partner can see things that his other partner can't, ain't that right, Abooksigun?"

The Algonquin Indian frowned at Immanuel. He knew he was being drawn into one of their arguments, and he didn't like it.

The question hung in the air for a while, then he answered, "Yes, no two braves see same."

"Okay, old man, what ya drivin' at?" Uzziah asked.

"I don't know really, it's just—well, ya saw how when we was out in the field how the soldiers near Stonewall kneel around his horse in the throes of battle."

"Yeah, is this about Obadiah?"

"No, no it ain't, it's 'bout the man their kneelin' round," Immanuel said, and pulling out his pipe, thoughtfully stuffed it, brought it afire, then let it go out, tamped it down, and lit it for good.

The others usually followed whoever pulled out their pipe first, and by the time Immanuel was puffing away with pleasure, the other two were also smoking.

"You were sayin'?" Uzziah started it back up.

"You got this—I don't know what to call it, but it's a leanin' toward some strange and dangerous people."

"Stonewall's dangerous?" Uzziah said, a big smile on his face. "Ya think the man who prays more than anyone I ever saw is dangerous?"

"Yes, yes, I do," Immanuel said.

"Why, pray tell?"

"I can't remember where I heard this, but it's one of those sayings that sticks with ya. '*It has been said that there is nothing more terrible than a band of brigands led by a cutthroat commander, except it be a group of Scottish Presbyterians rising from their knees in prayer about to go out and do what they see to be the will of God.*'" Immanuel even threw in a bit of Scottish brogue to fit the quotation.

"Ya read too much," Uzziah said and poured himself another cup of coffee.

"Is that all ya got to say, young son, have I not taught ya better. This man, this *MAN* is not God!"

"I know that!" Uzziah said, raising his voice.

"Do ya? What about Porter Rockwell?"

"For Christ's sake, he's the marshal in Salt Lake City, excuse me, Father," he finished up and looked toward the heavens.

"Yeah, now he is, but when ya was hangin' with him, what did ya do?"

"I got married, my wife died in childbirth—"

"Not those things, the magic stuff," Immanuel said.

"Ya mean 'bout being immune from shot and knife?" Uzziah said, looking puzzled.

"It's a story as old as the Greeks and as new as the Bard," Immanuel continued.

"Ya don't know what yer talkin' 'bout?"

"I do, I do. Achilles was said to be immune from death because his mother dipped him in a sacred pool, which was supposed to protect him from all harm, but she had to hold him by his heels as a child, and it was the arrow in his heel that eventually killed him! In the play whose name most thespians will not say—"

"Macbeth?" Uzziah said, knowing it would get under Immanuel's skin.

"Yes, the Scottish play. In that play, the witches—evil people—tell the man whose name ya just said that he cannot be killed by any man born of woman."

"I remember," Uzziah said thoughtfully.

"And do ya remember who kilt him?"

"MacDuff."

"Right, and how did he do it, if no man born of woman could kill that king and his murderous wife?"

"The doctors had taken Macduff by cutting him out of his mother's body, she didn't deliver him naturally, he was not born of woman, but what does any of this have to do with Stonewall?"

"Abooksigun?" Immanuel turned to his Algonquin friend.

"Hum?"

"Ever know any chiefs that thought they was untouchable?"

"Many braves have visions, no arrow or bullet can harm them, or the pony they ride."

"And then, what happens to them?"

"They die," Abooksigun said, hoping that was the last of him being dragged into the argument.

"And do they die old and alone?" Immanuel pressed his native friend.

"No, young in battle, many with them."

"This is a war, a civil war as they're callin' it," Uzziah said.

"Yeah, yeah, but the carnage, the carnage. I ain't seen no other animal kill its own kind like this, as a matter of fact, what it reminds me of is the buffalo run we went on. Notions, ideas, and haranguing men and pompous speeches have driven all of us up on this bluff, and it is a bluff. Who cares whether there's slaves or not? Who cares if the federal government wants to run things? Men will always seek power. Don't ya see, Uzziah, we are being driven and corralled into the narrow openings which can only lead us to the edge of the cliffs.

"This Civil War is the worst thing that's happened to man since Cain killed Abel. How many have to be slaughtered while the bands play on, and honor is talked about? How many? It's an ill wind that blows no good, and this wind stinks of corpses and putrefaction, my friend. Let's go back to our cabins in the Rockies, where only the bears and pumas are looking to kill us, and that's only when we cross 'em."

Uzziah was looking down at his hands for the last of what Immanuel had to say. He knew, he did, in his heart of hearts, that all this killing would end badly. Brother against brother, awful apocalyptic, really, but something still stirred in him, and he didn't know it at the time, but that something was the same thing that burned in his sister Hanna's heart. They had laid their youngest brother to grave, and outwardly he looked fine, but his spirit had flown, and deep in his ancestral bones, Uzziah thought someone had to pay. It was as simple as that.

Uzziah looked at Abooksigun.

"Don't look at me. People like me killin' each other since God made us."

"I think imma gonna leave this mess and go somewheres where life and death at least make sense," Immanuel said.

"I understand, partner. It weren't yer brother who was kilt, I understand," Uzziah said, and strangely he felt a swelling in his chest. He didn't want Immanuel to go, and if he did, he wanted to be going with him, but how, how could he? His other brothers and his pa were part of this!

"Good, 'cause I think I'm done with fanatics, and men who sit in harm's way and think they can't be kilt," Immanuel said as he knocked the dottle from the pipe into his open hand, then let it slip to the ground.

11

Orders were issued before General Lee's entourage had completely left the camp. Those orders were shouted out to inferior officers who shouted them out to their battalions. Some twelve hundred men mounted up, and along with them, Private John O'Bannon, aka Hanna O'Bannon.

"Is this it, then?" she asked Sergeant Stark, whom she bunked with, and with whom she felt like she might be inextricably falling for.

"Yes, private, this is it," Stark said, and his smile was as big as the morning sky.

"Where are we goin'?" O'Bannon asked.

"Well, as you like to put it, we're gonna kill some Yankees!"

Hanna's heart was filled. This was the moment she had been waiting for, to even the scales between what the Federals had taken from her family and to wreak vengeance on Yankees. She would kill as many as she could find in front of her new Walker Colt or carbine. She was ready.

It was to be a reconnaissance mission, Lee needed to know the true strength of McClellan's army and their relative position to Richmond, and it was only through such cavalry endeavors that that could be done.

Once J.E.B. Stuart was mounted up, something filled Hanna's heart which she had never felt before. There was her commander, her general! He was dressed as he always was when he went out with his troops. His cape with the red lining, his famous hat with the ostrich plume in it, wrinkling in the wind, his knee-high cavalry boots, and of course that infectious smile which existed right under his beard. These men loved him, and it was this love, the love which now Hanna, herself, was feeling for Stuart, which allowed him to extract from his men the extra mile, the extra effort that was needed to complete any mission.

In the early morning hours, as false dawn was breaking the horizon, Stuart and his twelve hundred men mounted on their war horses and quietly left the outskirts of Richmond, which the Federal army had every intention of invading.

As the day progressed, Stuart had most of the information which General Lee wanted to know, but Stuart wanted to pinpoint the Army of the Potomac's other flank, and in order to do that, he would have to ride around, completely around McClellan's army.

On the first day, they encountered no resistance other than scaring the heck out of several scouts and forward-placed pickets as they rode upon them, but did not engage.

As they began to circle the Army of the Potomac, General Phillip St. George Cooke, the head of the Federal cavalry, took off after Stuart's Cavalry. This was fine by Stuart since the man was none other than his father-in-law.

It had angered Jeb Stuart so much at the beginning of the war that his wife's father did not join the Confederacy, but chose instead to fight for the North, that he had sent a message to his wife, telling her to immediately change the name of their newborn son from that of her father's name to his name, and make him a junior. So it was that Jeb Stuart's first child began his life with the name Phillip St. George Stuart, but which was shortly changed to J.E.B. Stuart Jr.

And yet, this perfect circumambulation of the Federals was only spoiled on the afternoon of the second day of the ride around, when Stuart's Cavalry encountered Federal pickets in a brief hand-to-hand fight with them.

Hanna was thrilled when the pickets began firing at them, and Jeb turned his men right into their position. The pickets were mounted, and probably part of his father-in-law's cavalry, and possibly that was what encouraged Stuart not to back down.

The clashing of swords and the firing of pistols reigned supreme. Hanna, not being used to using a sword, used her Walker Colt, which was a repeating five-shot pistol, and emptied it, hitting three of the pickets she was aiming at and missing two. Two of the three she shot as they brazenly came at her with their swords ready to strike as they flew backward off their horses, and the third simply crumpled on his horse and rode away.

Her attention was on what she was doing, and when she turned to see where Stark was, she saw that he had been hit along the side of the head, and the wound was bleeding profusely. She rode up toward where he was as another of the pickets came at Stark with a sword to run him through. Without thinking, she simply ran Mandy into the side of the sword-wielding Federal and knocked him and his horse over into a tumbling and confused mass on the ground.

Riding up alongside Stark, she jumped from Mandy onto his horse, and taking the reins from his failing hands, she guided his horse along with those of Stuart's command who were continuing on their way.

They had retrieved the only mortally wounded man, one Captain William Latane of the 9th Virginia, and seemed to be proceeding somewhere with the body. She followed them, and Mandy, being the good horse she was, followed Hanna, riding behind Stark and guiding his horse without any problem.

While Stuart's men were digging the grave for the captain in the front yard of the Hanover Mansion, Hanna rode Stuart's horse to the back of the mansion, where there were slave quarters. She wasn't sure where she was going when a negro slave opened the door to a large barn and signaled her to ride in. Once she, Stark, and Mandy were inside, the slave closed the doors.

"What ya need, missy?" the slave asked. He was old and gray, and for a negro to be that gray, she knew he might just be ancient.

"Hot water, rags, and any medicine ya might find," Hanna asked.

"Yes, sirra, I fetch those presently," the man said as he left the barn through a man door.

She could hear the command firing their weapons in a salute to the fallen captain, then she could hear garbled orders shouted out, and Jeb Stuart's Cavalry rode from the Hanover Mansion, and fairly soon, she heard no more. The sun was low, and the deep shadows created by the tall live oaks fell upon the barn.

The main door opened, and she pointed the now reloaded Walker Colt at the old negro, who took no mind of it.

"They's bringin' hot water," he said as he picked up the passed-out Sergeant Stark and walked toward a tack room. Hanna opened the door for him, and the room was very pleasant. Perhaps it was the old negro's room, who knew? He placed the sergeant on the bed, and she could hear others out in the bigness of the barn whispering. When she looked out, there were several negress slaves, and they were filling a water trough with the hot water, then they brought some in for her.

"We's gotta stay clear, understand," the old man said as he placed the medicines and gauzes he had brought and left the tack room.

Hanna took the rags and, dipping them into the hot water, she wiped away the blood from the wound on Stark's head. She was relieved to find that it was only a graze. The bullet had driven a small valley along the left side of his head, right below his cap, and all the blood was from that deep scratch.

As she was working on him, he awakened.

"What? Where? Who are you?" he finally asked Hanna, and as she was about to explain, he slipped from consciousness again.

Hanna had known of a case like this back home in the Shenandoah Valley. A man who had lived two farms down had fallen off his barn roof, and when he came to, his head bleeding badly, he walked into town and gotten drunk at the local store. When his wife found him, he had a young girl sitting on his lap, and he was in the middle of telling a story about the life he thought he was living. The wife had grabbed him by the ear and took him home, where days later he regained his rightful memory.

Hanna wondered if this—what had happened to the man she was trying so desperately not to fall in love with—if this was something similar. In his short-awakened period, he had seemed totally disoriented and not sure who she was.

She bandaged the groove in his head by putting iodine on it and winding the bandages around his head, splitting the bandage and tying it off. By the time she had finished, it was dark, and only the moonlight from what seemed a full moon was easing its way through all the cracks and crannies in the old barn's roof.

Several of the stalls had mules in them, and Hanna realized that this wasn't the main barn, but the place where the slaves kept the stock that helped them do their jobs.

As she passed the water trough where the women had brought the hot water, she, without thinking, ran her hand through the water. It was deliciously warm. How long had it been since she had had a bath?

As if her hands had a mind of their own, she was undressing and letting her cavalry uniform fall to the floor of the barn. She unwound her breasts, which had been bound up for God knows how long. Her body stank as she slipped into the trough. Along the side, there was a bar of tallow which she imagined the negroes used to bathe with. She didn't care, she just wanted to be clean.

She scrubbed herself until she felt fresh, then lay back in the warm water, and she must have gone to sleep. She was awakened by a male voice.

"Where am I? Hello, is anybody there?" It was Stark, and he had left the tack room and was wandering out into the barn on his way to the man door.

"I'm here," she said as she stood from the tub. She wasn't sure what that meant, only that she had to keep him from going outside since later in the afternoon, the Federal cavalry had arrived and were camped around the Hanover Mansion.

He turned and looked at her, streams of water were running down her, making silken rivulets highlighted by the moonlight. Her shape, the voluptuous curves of her breasts, the flatness of her muscled stomach, and her round hips and thighs spoke to him. He walked toward her.

She was captivated, it was like when a shunted lantern is pointed toward a deer at night. She froze there, almost holding her breath.

"Who are you?" he asked, not in a threatening way.

She knew then that his memory loss continued, and what she said next, she never dreamed of saying, nor would she have if not for the circumstances.

"I'm your wife, Hanna," she said breathlessly as the moonlight played on her reddish short hair and glistened in the drops on her skin.

"My wife?" he said flatly, then added, "What's yer name, again?"

"Hanna."

"I...I don't remember," he said as he walked closer.

"There was a hunting accident, and you're wounded," Hanna said.

He reached up and touched the bandage.

"My head hurts," he said, and she shivered from the dampness on her body.

"Here," he said, and picking her up, carried her back to the bunk in the tack room. "Lay here and I'll keep ya warm," he said.

As she lay on the bunk, he undressed, and she was not disappointed. All she had hoped was under those clothes, what she had always thought she'd seen him in, was there, and then some.

He lay down beside her and took her damp body into his arms and pulled her close to him. Yes, he smelled musky and not clean, but she had smelled worse on men, and she did not care. They lay there a bit, then his manhood awakened and pushed against her thigh.

"Oops," he said.

She reached over and, taking him by the back of the neck, pulled his face closer to hers, and then, the moment she had been waiting for, their lips met, and once again, she was not disappointed. In fact, the longer they kissed and the more their tongues acted like otters in a pool, the heavier her breath became, and so did his. He pulled himself on top of her, and she reached down, and even though it was her first time, she knew how it should be and where. She placed it there, and he was amazingly gentle as he took her cherry, and slowly they made love.

When he finished, her back arched upward, and she drew every ounce of him inside her. She wanted his seed, and she took it. He rolled beside her, enclosing her in his arms, and they fell immediately asleep.

In the morning, she heard his voice. It had returned to the voice of the sergeant, not the voice of her lover from the night before.

"O'Bannon," he said, then repeated it, "Private John O'Bannon!?"

"Here," Hanna said. She had bound herself up again and was dressed as her dead brother.

He was standing in the doorway to the tack room and was, more or less, dressed.

"What happened?" The same question he'd asked the night before.

"You were wounded, I brought you in here, the negroes helped me dress your wounds," she said as she continued to feed Mandy and the sergeant's horse.

He reached up just as he had last night and felt the wound.

"They did a good job, I should thank them," he said as he walked toward the main door.

"Wait, there's Union cavalry out there," she whispered.

He went to the door and gazed through the cracks.

"Oh my God," he said.

"Don't worry, I've been listening, they're about to mount up, then we can leave," she said.

They did have long to wait, but as they sat there in the tack room waiting, he looked at her a couple of times, and she thought for sure that he was remembering. After all, the bed, the bunk where they had done what they had done, was right there. He opened his mouth as if to speak, then shut it.

"You were about to say something?" she asked.

"Ah, it was nothin'," he said.

They could hear the Union cavalry's orders. Their mounting up and leaving. They waited another twenty minutes, then, saddling up, mounted their horses, and Stark reached down and lifted the log lock on the barn doors, and they rode out into the morning sunshine. Looking around, they realized it was safe now.

"How will we ever catch up with them?" Hanna asked.

"We'll just go back to the camp north of Richmond, they'll show up," he said as they rode off in that direction.

He turned and looked at Private O'Bannon, then shook his head.

"What is it?" she asked.

"I had the weirdest dream last night," he said, smiling.

"By your smile, it must have been pleasant," Hanna said.

"Oh, it was, but I'm too much a gentleman to relate it," he said as he kicked his horse up into a lope.

As they rode toward Richmond, Hanna was glad he hadn't made light of it, told the dream to a mere boy, even if she were the boy. It meant...what did it mean? It meant that on some level, what had happened between them, even as a dream, meant as much to him as it certainly did to her. She couldn't help but smile.

And yet a niggling sensation came from deep within her. *No good thing comes from a lie.* It was something her mother had instilled in all the girls. Nothing good could come from practicing the art of the prince of the power of the air. After all, wasn't he considered the father of all lies, and wasn't his kingdom of hell built on deception and subterfuge?

She shook her head and felt the wind in her face. She would stop thinking like that, she would. It was an innocent enough bending of the truth. What could possibly come from such innocence? She set her eyes on Stark as he rode just a bit ahead of her, and she wondered if deep down he knew what had happened. Surely, he didn't, and yet, she wanted him to know that he had known her. Oh, she did have a way of making things more complicated than they had to be, didn't she?

"You all right, Cavalryman?" Stark asked, he'd turned to the boy only to see a worried look on the boy's face.

"I'm fine, just fine, glad yer feeling better," Hanna said.

"Well, if it hadn't been fer you, I wouldn't be, and I'm going to be sure and tell J.E.B. Stuart about it when we join up with them. I think maybe you're going to be called Corporal from now on," he said, smiling, then looked over the head of his horse.

Great, she had lain with her boss and was being promoted! How in the world did things come to this? she wondered.

A LOOK AT BOOK NINE: DEATH TO DESERTERS
A UZZIAH MOUNTAIN MAN WESTERN DOUBLE

War pulls them in. Madness follows close behind.

Uzziah O'Bannon and Immanuel Jones return to the Civil War, scouting for the Confederacy and rounding up deserters with help from an Algonquin tracker. But when Stonewall Jackson's justice proves harsher than expected, Immanuel's had enough. He heads west—only to discover Hanna O'Bannon, disguised as her dead brother in Jeb Stuart's cavalry. A gunshot wound, a desperate rescue, and a brutal turn at Chancellorsville convince them both it's time to leave the war behind.

Back in the West, peace proves just as dangerous. In St. Louis, the mountain men cross paths with a wealthy old man and his bold granddaughter, bound for Salt Lake City. When one of their hired guards ends up dead, Uzziah and Immanuel join the journey west, suspecting something's not right. By the time they reach Fort Laramie, a second body is found—and once in Utah, the trail of violence leads straight to Porter Rockwell and the Prophet himself, Brigham Young.

Can the mountain men stop what's coming? Or will one of them fall for a woman hiding more than just secrets?

This two-book bundle includes the seventeenth and eighteenth novels in the Uzziah Mountain Man Series.

AVAILABLE MARCH 2026

THANK YOU

Thank you for taking the time to read *Wolf Point: A Western Double*. If you enjoyed it, please consider telling your friends or posting a short review. Word of mouth is an author's best friend and much appreciated.

Thank you.
J.J. Bonham

ABOUT THE AUTHORS

He was good looking and could sell ice to eskimos. But ... writing asked something else from him. He would have to corral his interest in being free. Writing would take him to a place where he was tamed, but also able to actually tell a story.

After the first two weeks at the Yale School of Drama, he called the head of the playwriting department, Milan Stitt and told him he was quitting. Milan invited him to lunch at a nearby Mexican restaurant in New Haven. He told the man who had had plays on Broadway that he wanted to be a free writer. Milan smiled, then explained the way to freedom was always through discipline.

Something in him clicked and it all began to make sense.

Three years later, when he received his MFA in playwriting, he received the much coveted Cole Porter Prize for Excellence in Writing.

Enter a woman, years later, when the first 'J' in J.J. Bonham, Jack Bonham, had written thirty screenplays in 7 years and had one optioned which looked like it actually might be done.

Unlike Milan Stitt, this woman had no plays on Broadway, but was a divorced mother of four grown children. She loved soaps, and was an ardent watcher of the same. In the years of her devotion to watching she developed an uncanny ability to discern plot and analyze character. Uncanny, really better than any of his teachers at Yale.

They, Jack & Judy, the other 'J' in J.J. Bonham, married in Buffalo Springs, Colorado. While teaching elementary school in Denver they read the same novella and looking up and into each other's eyes, realizing something. They could do that.

Thirteen years later they had written nearly 200 novels. Westerns mostly because that was who they were – a misplaced couple from the 19th Century who saw life in a western justice sort of way. They danced in Virgina City, Montana. Dances from a different time and place, but still their time and place.

Now, they live in the Bitterroot Valley on five acres and looking out the office window as he puts this together for them, he can see the thunderstorm marching across the Sapphire Mountains. Earlier, sitting on the porch, she had said something about the crack of lightning years before as they said vows of love in Buffalo Springs. He remembered.

www.ingramcontent.com/pod-product-compliance
Lightning Source LLC
LaVergne TN
LVHW040217110826
845146LV00005B/1323

* 9 7 9 8 8 9 5 6 7 3 5 9 1 *